HERO FROM THE SEA

"From the sea an hero comes."

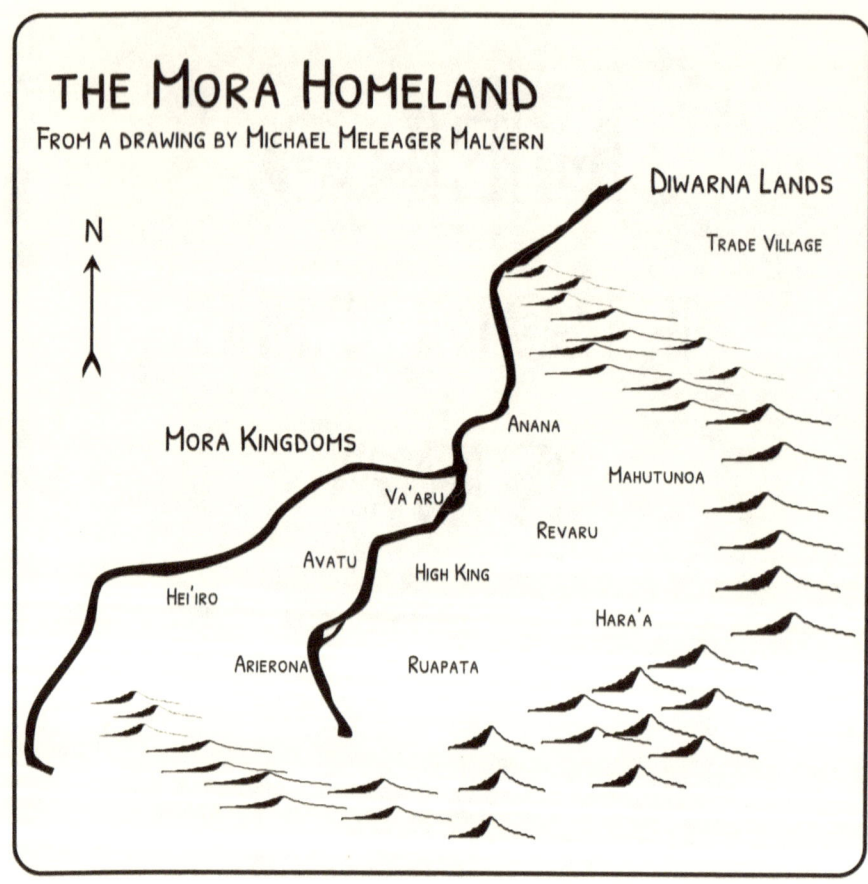

THE MORA HOMELAND

FROM A DRAWING BY MICHAEL MELEAGER MALVERN

N

DIWARNA LANDS

TRADE VILLAGE

MORA KINGDOMS

Anana

Mahutunoa

Va'aru

Revaru

Avatu

High King

Hei'iro

Hara'a

Arierona

Ruapata

Hero from the Sea

Stephen Brooke

Arachis Press 2016
AP

Hero from the Sea
©2016 Stephen Brooke

ISBN 978-1-937745-31-8

Arachis Press
4803 Peanut Road
Graceville, FL 32440
http://arachispress.com

Part I. The Way Home

1. A Door

"I think I miss doors," said Rahaita.

"Another noble savage ruined by civilization," said I, rolling over to behold my bride. The pale light of dawn filtered in, through and around the grass mat walls. She had no idea what I was talking about.

My bride. Perhaps the Mora would not recognize her as being such, surely her father, King Arierona, would not, but we had stood before the shaman Oorto, my best friend in this and any other world, yesterday and made our vows. Of course, the Mora people have little objection to lovemaking outside of marriage so our status would not actually matter to most of them.

"I'll build you doors if you wish them," I told her. "Or get Dutch to do it. Dutsa. The people here call him Dutsa." Dutch Geitz, former engineer of the quite unlucky "Double Lucky" yacht had made his abode in this little trading town on the border between Mora and Diwarna lands.

"They call him Gaho now, Marareta." I had to think a moment about the meaning of the word in her language. The clever one, right? Fitting enough. She giggled. "Some even call him Taona Gaho."

"Oh?" I didn't quite know what to think of that; up until now I had been the only one of our castaways to receive that honorific title. "Should I be jealous?"

"No, my husband. Your wife is far more beautiful than his." I had to fully agree with this. In fact, I decided there was absolutely no reason to rise and leave that wife yet.

"Are you awake?" came a whisper from outside.

"No!" I answered. "Go away, Heho." The courier could not have helped but hear us, so there was no use in pretending sleep.

"The Lady Pua only wished to let you know that messengers are on their way to Arierona and to her son. The Lady Rahaita's father will be overjoyed to learn she is safe."

I kissed Rahaita, rolled over, and rose. "Hold," I called and stepped outside the hut to talk with the man. "They are already on their way?" I had hoped to add to those messages.

"They are, Taona," he replied. It was good to see his friendly, flat face after all these months. "Do we need to send another courier? If there is something of great import I shall go myself."

"No, no, my friend. There is nothing that can not wait." I glanced at Rahaita, emerging to join us. "Did the messages include, um, mention of our marriage?"

"They did not." Heho smiled widely. "Pua thought it might be too much good news."

"I would that he had been told," spoke Rahaita. "There can be no return to A'auwa until I know he approves." She looked up at me — only a very short way up, as Rahaita was nearly my own height — saying, "I would not have him think you stole me, as did Nezama."

I nodded in agreement. "I think," said Heho, turned quite serious now, "as does Pua, that the king will simply ignore your marriage. You know he is a traditionalist — if the wedding was not performed by the old rites, it does not exist for him."

"Then we shall have to have another wedding at the house of Arierona," I declared. "I missed not having a feast at this one."

"I should be feast enough," my wife told me. Turning to Heho, she asked, "Will Pua wish to see us today?" We had greeted her briefly on first arriving at this village, but had seen little of the Mora noblewoman since.

"That is the second half of my message," he replied. "The Lady Pua wishes you to attend her later this morning." Heho chuckled. "You may get your wedding feast then."

Pua always laid a good spread. I was not sure why she was here at this little trading post, however, instead of with her son, the newly crowned High King. This did not seem a particularly good time to pump Heho for information, as we stood in the damp early morning air. Later maybe.

Or Pua would tell us herself.

"Have you seen Oorto this morning?" I asked him.

"He is with Ulani, of course. They'll come up for air eventually. His sister is here somewhere and the rest of your people."

I knew the remainder of my party, my fellow castaways, had been sent here for their safety. That I had learned on arriving, though I had seen only some of them, for a few moments. Moreover, Rahaita had glimpsed them here in a vision, while on the far side of those high, distant mountains we had recently crossed. Perhaps that was why Lady Pua, too, was here.

"We'll have to visit them," said I. "But first, let us find some breakfast. Hungry?" I asked Rahaita.

"I could eat all day," she answered, and it was probably true. We had been on short rations for far too long.

"Come with me, then," said Heho. "I can lead you to both food and your friends."

There were already traders setting up along the main way through the village. I suppose one could call it a street. Most of what went on here was the exchange of goods between the Mora and Diwarna, woven mats, crocodile hides, and such coming south from the valley of Gurang, and cloth, vessels of carved wood, and a host of other craft-goods being brought across the hills from the Mora homeland. To our left stood the home of Lady Pua — or whoever the Mora representative here was at any given time.

"What became of Ma'are?" I asked Heho. She had been in charge when we left to cross the mountains. A widowed niece of Pua, I believed she was.

"She still runs things, for the most part," he replied. "Pua is too busy with what is going on across the hills." Meaning in the Mora realm. "Ma'are and I are to be married," he added, rather nonchalantly. I had known Heho the courier to find female companionship wherever his duties took him. Was he settling down here?

"You shouldn't wait," Rahaita advised him, wrinkling her nose at me. You needn't tell me, my girl.

"Each thing in its time," came his philosophical reply. "It is near the time I no longer spent my days running here and there with other people's words."

A low, open, thatch-roofed building, as were many here, lay before us and there a great many Mora were partaking of a buffet — pretty much the standard way in which that people served their meals. Pua's entourage and traveling traders shared this breakfast, and with them were most of those who had been castaway here with me. So long ago it seemed now! With them, too, were those who had accompanied me over the mountains and back.

All save Oorto. He would show up eventually. Would he make his way back to the Diwarna swamps and jungles now, to be the greatest shaman that land had ever known? I glanced at the girl by my side; one might ask similar questions of her.

Ah, well. As Heho said, each thing in its time. Now was the time for food and gossip.

2. Changes

When I began boxing, I was a skinny lad with a reach advantage over most of my opponents but little power to back it up. For a time, I was not willing to give up the advantage, put on some muscle, and move up a class. I was clinging to that one sure thing I knew I had.

I learned. It took a beating or two but, yes, I learned. I learned there are times when we must take a chance and leave what is comfortable behind. Just as I later left the ring behind to take up painting. It took me a while to learn that lesson anew, here on this lost coast, in this unknown world.

Then again, perhaps it is in my nature to move on to the next thing. If not, I would still be on a hay farm, cursing the automobile and the diminishing demand for my crop. That I left to my brothers.

Be that as it may, I had taken the chance, gained the weight, left the farm, picked up the paint brush. Then I had again become set in my ways, sticking with what I knew, playing the society portrait painter, playing it safe. Until I had agreed to accompany James L. Nathan and his family, cruising the South Seas on his private yacht, and ended up here.

But it took me a while to fully learn my lesson, even here, and be willing to reach out, take a chance, and win the woman who now walked beside me. I would never be reluctant to let Rahaita know how I felt about her. Not now.

Here were those who had been on that yacht with me. I took a seat beside James Nathan — by which I mean I sat on the ground next to him — with Rahaita by me. There was no Mora protocol about who sat where, in this place. I looked at the faces of those gathered around their morning meal and was gladdened to once again see them.

But George Bath was not there. I pondered his loss with heavy heart. "Would that George had lived to be with us here today," I sighed.

"Yes," agreed Rahaita, "Bafa was very brave when Nezama took me."

J.L. Nathan was pleased to be able to correct me. "Oh, the boy pulled through and is doing splendidly — thanks in part to Amelia's nursing." He nodded toward where his daughter sat, picking at some fruit. Several young Mora men seemed to be paying her close attention, my comrade Aranu among them. "Arierona was so taken with the boy's courage that he adopted him as his son. That is why he is not here with the rest of us. Princely duties!"

Rahaita smiled. "Bafa, my brother — I do not think I mind that."

"Now they don't know which of you is the promised hero," Nathan went on. "Odds had been on you, but Bath's stock has gone up considerably." He gave me an appraising look. "I suspect it will be your turn again."

"Oh, he is quite welcome to the title," I told him. "I just want a hut by the river and my wife." I leaned over to kiss Rahaita, but her mouth was full of yams. "Later," I whispered.

She nodded agreeably and kept chewing.

"Yes, congratulations on that, my boy. You will have to give us the story of your journey sometime. We've had bits and pieces of it already from your companions."

"Ulani will want to make an epic of it, to sing across the Mora realm," stated Heho. "He is probably getting Oorto's version of things even now."

"As good a version as any," said I. "I fear Oorto is not the same boy who left Ulani here all those months ago."

"Nor is Ulani the same. This place will no longer hold him." Heho turned his attention to some dried fish. Then he looked up and grinned. "I do not think Lady Pua has any interest in you as a husband now."

Rahaita glared at him for a moment. "She'd better not," she declared, and started on her fourth yam.

Nathan told me, "Your Pua suggested I take a second wife. I fear Judith would not approve at all."

"Zu-dif?" whispered Rahaita to me.

"Hueta," I whispered back. "Neatanu still isn't used to calling her by her Mora name." I, on the other hand, didn't think to use anything but those Mora names now. I could put such names to most of the crew and passengers of the "Double Lucky." Hmm, not the two we had rescued from the Kohari and had become Nathan's retainers. I don't think I ever heard Mora names for them. I looked from one face to another, before realizing that another was missing.

"What has become of Samua?" I asked. "Samuel." Samuel had been the half-Chinese cook whom I later took on as my personal attendant. Neither young enough nor in good enough shape, he had not accompanied me on my recent journeys.

"He got religion," spoke old Andrew Bailey, Nathan's longtime steward and known now as Andarua.

"He already had religion," James L. said, "but now religion has him."

Andrew laughed at that. I didn't get the joke. "He joined those priests who live on the island. The one just above the falls."

"At least he never has to worry about falling off the wagon again," remarked J.L. Nathan.

"More likely to fall in the lake," was Andrew's reply. "But I think it's a good place for him. Most of 'em never leave that rock."

"Well, maybe I'll visit him when we return." I turned to Rahaita. "Is that permitted?"

"I am not sure," she admitted. "No one wants to visit there. And it is dangerous to take a canoe so close to the falls. They only receive supplies once each moon."

"None of us will be going back until things settle down," Nathan said. He smoothed his dark beard and continued. "We hear rumors and tales and don't know which to believe. Pua doesn't really keep us informed, assuming she knows herself."

"It is the priests," claimed Heho, "stirring things up. Some of them. The kings who opposed Ve'eta are not sure which way to jump now."

"So, not war yet?"

HERO FROM THE SEA

"No, not yet."

"It will come," murmured Rahaita. "I have seen it."

3. Out of the Basket

"Have you ever heard the original prophecy of the hero from the sea, Taona Marareta?" asked the Lady Pua. "Mmm, this melon is excellent."

"I can not say that I have, my lady," I replied, glancing sidelong at Rahaita. I assumed it would be known to her and, indeed, she immediately gave it to us.

Brother wars upon his brother;
in his house the High King trembles.
From the sea an hero comes
to restore the peaceful kingdom.

"That seems a bit slender to hang much importance on it," I observed.

"Ah, but it was spoken as true prophecy and, so, must be taken seriously," Rahaita replied.

Pua concurred. "Were it unimportant, Taona, it would not have come in a vision. The same is true of the more recent seeing of Pana'a, the one we believe told of you."

She looked toward Rahaita, who recited this one for us as well.

On the world's edge, a sail —
comes the hero once foretold.
Soon the crown will fall to earth;
soon the crown will rise again.

"Yes," said Pua, nodding her head. "This could have meant the death of Maitoa and the ascension of my son, as has come to pass, or it could mean the fall of our house and the rise of a new dynasty.

"We must seek a new prophecy from Pana'a," she declared. Long and thoughtful was the look that Rahaita and I gave each other. She, too, could prophecy now and was perhaps a more powerful seer than her aunt. Pua need not know this, though I was certain that tales of the gift must have reached her ears by this time.

Rahaita's visions would not come out in neat verses, however. That was certainly a function of the trance state entered by the priestesses.

The girl looked out over the town and then back at the breakfast — or perhaps early lunch — spread upon Pua's veranda. "I would like to see my aunt again, soon, and Lake A'auwa and my father." She regarded me, her expression holding the hint of a smile. "I think you, as well, would wish to gaze upon Pana'a."

I was a bit surprised, even knowing the Mora's general lack of jealousy. "Did you not say Pana'a had a new lover?"

"No, Marareta, I told you she had a new man in her life." She did no more than continue to smile in a decidedly enigmatic manner.

But Pua laughed loudly. "He does not know?"

Rahaita laughed as well, and shook her head. "You may inform him, my lady. I am sure you have many more details than I."

Lady Pua seemed quite willing — indeed, happy — to deliver the news. "That man is your son. He was born while you were across the mountains."

A son. Rahaita knew. I suppose I stared at her as this all sank in.

"I thought it best to wait until we had left that valley before telling you, or even leave it up to Pana'a when we returned home. But," continued Rahaita, "our Lady Pua has let the cat out of the basket."

The Mora girl had not yet even seen a cat a year before but we had brought two back with us, yes, in baskets, and I had introduced the expression to my friends. They had quickly recognized its aptness.

I allowed them to believe I had come up with it myself.

"A cat?" asked Pua. "One of those little murderers you carried here?" The pair had been busy decimating the unwary local rodent population.

"Kaleea is in heat again," Rahaita said. "We may have let many cats out of the basket."

"Be that as it may," I answered, having regained the greater part of my composure. "One way or another, cats would have arrived in this land eventually. I would rather hear more of this other arrival, Lady Pua."

The Mora noblewoman drank deeply of her millet beer, before speaking. I had greatly missed that beer while beyond the mountains.

"I have not laid eyes upon the child but I have heard he is healthy and strong and as comely as his parents. She calls him

Mika, but that is only until a more proper name can be chosen. Being male, the baby is not permitted on the Sacred Island but he is well cared for in the house of Arierona. Your cousins are seeing to that, Rahaita."

Pua studied the younger woman rather intently for a few moments. "You knew of this when you were still beyond the mountains. So what I have heard of you is true." Her eyes turned southward, toward the homeland of her people. "It may be you are meant to take your aunt's place, in time."

That was something I most definitely did not want to happen.

"The two of you must return to the house of Arierona," Pua continued. "Again, in time. I would not send you without preparing the way. Rest for now." She smiled, but that smile held a trace of weariness. "And enjoy each other."

"Only we two return?" I asked.

"Your friends from the sea remain here. It is the safest place for them. Aranu, too — it would not be right to ask him to take sides if his father wars against my son."

"I shall ask him to stay and protect my people." I chuckled. "We can tell him it was Arierona's will."

Rahaita looked rather scandalized by this notion, but Pua laughed with me. "That I shall do, Taona. I shall send Heho with you, I think."

"No better man," I agreed.

4. Clay

"We seek clay, Taona."

I assumed that the two women addressed me, even if Dutch Geitz was also being called Taona these days. But it was Gordie who answered.

"It is mostly sand around here." He turned to his wife. "I've seen clay fire-floors in all the Diwarna villages. Do you know where it is found?"

Demba did not, only that it came from somewhere up the Gurang.

"Then there are traders who bring it," surmised Dutch. "But that is too far away to do these ladies any good."

"And it might not suitable for pottery," I added. Turning to Tala and Amlee, I said, "That is why you want it, I am sure." The pair had learned of pot making on the other side of the mountains, in the Valley of Visions, and brought the skill back along with their cats.

It was a skill neither Diwarna nor Mora possessed. Yes, the Mora made rudimentary pots and bowls, but being a people skilled in wood carving and basket making, they had not pursued that craft.

It was a craft that Dutch felt would be useful. "We'll just have to go looking for some," he decided. "Do you know how to use a wheel?"

"Yes, Gaho," replied Amlee, a full-blooded woman of the Diwarna who had accompanied her man across the mountains and back.

"We learned of it over there." She indicated those mountains with a movement of her head, without looking at them.

"Then I reckon I'll have to build one for you." The word, the very concept, of the wheel was unknown here until a year ago. Then Dutch had introduced the wheelbarrow, with the patronage of Ulani, Pua's right hand at that time.

In fact, there were barrows and carts currently under construction here in his workshop. I think he had yet to hit upon a combination of materials that completely satisfied him, but much use was made of bamboo.

"I heard Kaleea and Ulap carrying on all last night," I said, changing the subject.

Tala grinned broadly. "We will have more cats soon!"

"You will have to keep them from wandering. A mabi would not hesitate to eat one." That was an occasionally spied, medium-sized, tawny wildcat of these savannas. It seemed lynx-like to me.

"The dogs do not like them either," said Amlee.

"They have never seen cats before," Tala told her. "They are like wandering tribes that meet for the first time, each thinking they are the sole possessors of the land." I was surprised to hear the normally shy woman wax so poetic. And so astute.

Few dogs were kept at the trade village; it was different over the hills in the Mora homeland. There, they were common and sometimes served as food. I had steadfastly refused to partake of that fare.

"Here comes my brother," spoke Demba. "Oorto might know where to find clay. He has been all over. We were never able to keep him home, even as a small boy!"

With the young shaman walked his lover. Ulani had reportedly pined deeply for Oorto while they had been separated, spending his time composing songs, no longer being the man who had run this town for the Mora. But in that time both men had matured, one becoming a powerful shaman, indeed, a sorcerer, and the other finally embracing his training and talent as a storyteller. Their paths, I felt, would inevitably part.

But they were together now, and happy. That was good. I was in a mood to wish everyone happiness.

Demba hugged her brother, and then Ulani. "Greetings, my Poa'ave," said he.

Poa'ave? A Mora name, but I could not quite puzzle out the meaning. Black-something, I thought. My ignorance must have shown. "It means *Black Pearl*," whispered Gordie. "He's been calling Demba that for quite some time." The boy smiled at the pair. "If he weren't a poof, I might be jealous of the time he has spent with her." This was in English. We all, of course, had been conversing in the pidgin, not in Mora.

"Do you know of any clay deposits around here, Oorto?" he then asked his brother-in-law. "The closer, the better."

The Diwarna thought for only a moment. "I've seen none between here and the Gurang. But a half-day walk in, hmm, that direction —" He pointed more or less to the west. "There is a tribe that likes to decorate itself with daubs of white clay. I have seen where they gather it."

"We'll have to take gifts," decided Gordie, apparently taking charge of the expedition. Gordon Watkins, the unsure boy who had shipped on the "Double Lucky," had become a leader of men in this land.

As he organized those men — and women — I ambled back to my own hut and my own bride. Pua wanted to see me again today, me only, but I was not going to be hurried about it. The politics of the Mora nation, across the hills, meant little to me right now.

5. Matches

"I will need another tattoo, now I am a married woman," Rahaita told me. She looked me over. "You need some too."

My only ink consisted of a small heart with my mother's name that I had picked up in Buffalo, when young, stupid, and drunk. Rahaita, as all her people, carried many tattoos on her body. She was young, so there was still lots of room for additions.

Unlike the Lady Pua, who was adorned from neck to foot. I knew from, ah, personal experience, that all parts of her were covered with designs.

"I have no clan or family whose symbols I might wear," I told her.

"There are marks that are only for those who serve the gods," was her reply. It was true these people saw me as a sort of priest. "Is that sign on your arm such?"

"Only if one serves the god of love, I suppose."

Rahaita approved of that. "The best of all gods." She came close and looked at the heart. "Is it some sort of fruit?" She peered again. "No, a leaf!"

Why not? "A leaf that never falls." I thought it sounded good.

She nodded her head, seeming to understand completely. "I want a leaf, too. Maybe, mmm, here." She pointed to an empty spot on her left breast — a rather appropriate spot for a heart. Then she hugged me, saying, "Off to Pua's house with you, to make your secret plans. But be sure to tell them all to me when you return."

HERO FROM THE SEA

Pua seemed more worn, thinner even, than when I had seen her more than half a year past. Not that the Mora noble was in any way a slight woman. She stood my height and certainly still outweighed me. Yet events *had* taken their toll. We lunched privately in a shaded corner of her porch.

"I must think of alliances, Marareta," she told me. "I do not object to your marriage to Rahaita but it serves no political end." She sighed and idly picked up a slice of papaya, only to replace it. "If I had my way, the daughter of Arierona would marry my son. Arierona also favors this."

"Rahaita has no desire to wed Ve'eta." I knew I could say that with certainty.

"I realize this. It would be an excellent match, however."

I asked, not at all seriously, "Isn't she allowed more than one husband?" Pua, of course, had two herself.

"It is not permitted. A wife of the High King may have no other husbands. Yes, I know that is cruel but it is the custom. Of course, there is no objection to a lover or two." She looked at me and shook her head. "I know that would not be enough for you. Nor for Rahaita. She is as hardheaded as her father, and as loyal."

Although I had been gone from these lands for some while, I had learned much of Mora marriage customs in my earlier time here. It was more commonly the nobles, the powerful, who engaged in polygamous relationships, and these were often a matter of politics and alliances.

Incidentally, each marriage is a separate contract between two individuals and has no bearing on any other spouse either might

24

have. I have heard of 'group marriages' among certain Bohemian societies back in the world from which I came, but no such thing existed here.

Pua went on. "Panoha and you would also be a good marriage." The woman she named was one the widows of her brother Maitoa, once High King of all the Mora, as well as the sister of our protector Hareata. Politically, it would be a good match — if I had any interest in politics.

I remembered Panoha, from my brief stay in the High King's house, and her offer to stay with me — purely a matter of Mora hospitality — the night an assassin had later crept into my room. A pleasant enough woman, and not unattractive. "That would tie one who might be the hero from the sea to your cause," I stated. "But I am not that hero."

"Maybe you are, maybe you are not." Pua chuckled. "You are not Pana'a, after all, and have not seen what will come."

"Rahaita has seen war."

Pua's eyes narrowed. "I hope she is not part of the cause."

I shrugged. "She has seen and her seeing is as true as her aunt's. This I believe."

"Then it will come. That is not unexpected." Lady Pua considered this. "The land is in turmoil, especially the northern kingdoms through which you must pass to reach Arierona. Many traders fear to cross the hills these days."

We gazed out on the village and sipped our beer for a minute or two. "It would be a good match for Panoha, too," Lady Pua said, returning to the topic of marriage. "She is no older than you and has nowhere to go save back to her brother. Few would be willing to take the widow of a High King, for fear of the political implications." She place her large, caramel-colored hand on my arm. "For you, that would be of little concern.

"Maybe, Marareta, you are the one who should have a second spouse."

6. Dreams

"You and Panoha?" Rahaita was not sure whether I was joking.

I asked, "Do you know her?"

"Once she came to my father's house with her brother. I was only a little girl then and she had not yet married Maitoa. Maybe Hareata hoped to match her with my father. She seemed — sweet but not very bright."

"Some men would consider that admirable," I told my wife, who gave me a menacing look. Ignoring that, I continued, "I believe Pua is genuinely concerned about her future."

We stood now by the spring-fed lake at the northern edge of the town, the reason this town was able to exist here in the bowl-shaped little valley. I gazed at the stream that ran from its far end, so small here one could step over it. "That stream eventually leads to the Gurang, an even mightier river than the Teoma you know. You have only seen the upper reaches of the Gurang, in the mountains."

"Neither is as great as the Tez," replied Rahaita. "Could it be the greatest river in the world?"

"Maybe. It is certainly the biggest I have seen." In this world, anyway. Might the Mississippi be larger? I put my arm around my wife. "You know," I began, "if you and Oorto had decided to stay with the Lord of Visions, I might not have come back either, but chosen to explore the length of Tez."

"You feared I might choose Hurasu over you?"

"Every day."

"But Marareta, that is silly. You know Pana'a foretold that we would be together."

I smiled at that. "And Pana'a is always right. As are you, my love." I was not going to ask how she knew of the prophecy. I had never told her.

"Would you like to see the Gurang again?" she asked me. "We do not have to travel south, if you do not wish it. We could live with Oorto in the swamp!" I could tell this was Rahaita's impish humor speaking. But I will not deny that I had thought of that very possibility.

"I would not keep you from your father," I told her. "And I wish to look upon A'auwa again, myself."

"Not to mention Pana'a and your son." She spoke still with a light, bantering tone but I knew the words were now serious.

"Yes," I agreed. "There is that."

"We must take the boy into our own household when we return." Rahaita fixed her eyes on a young man near by, standing gazing into the pond. He wore a poncho, coarsely woven of grass fiber, concealing most of his torso. But not all of it. "He has the tattoos of a priest," she whispered to me, nodding in the fellow's direction. "Why would he be here?"

And why would he attempt to conceal his identity? It would do to keep an eye on him, and maybe mention his presence to someone. Heho, maybe? "For no good reason, I would fear. He might be a spy."

She nodded her agreement. That made sense.

"Oorto tells me there is place of power along the way to the Gurang," she said, "and that you once dreamed there."

"Would you wish to visit it?" I asked.

"I can dream anywhere," said Rahaita. "I prefer to do it by your side." We turned and strolled back into the village. We did not see Heho but did run into Ma'are, whom we informed of our suspicions. She would relay them to Lady Pua, and Heho as well, most likely.

"She is related to Pua, isn't she?" I asked, after we parted.

"The widow of one of her nephews," came the reply. "Some would disapprove of her taking a commoner as husband now." She frowned. "Heho had better be good to her."

"I think she can keep him in line. Ma'are seems very competent." The two of them would probably be running this trade village for many years to come.

"She also seems pregnant," stated Rahaita. I hadn't noticed, but took her word for it. Ma'are was already rather round by nature.

What dreams had Rahaita now? This I wondered, as she slept beside me that night. She had not foretold anything since our arrival here. I did not know if she had exercised her powers at all, but knew she would not be able to resist using them eventually. Or visions might come to her unasked.

I had nearly fallen asleep again, lulled by her steady breathing, when a loud sound rang out. It took me a moment to recognize it for what it was — gunfire!

But I had thrown the Krag rifle aside, beyond the mountains, when it was no longer of use, all our ammunition expended and no more to be found in this world. It could only be the shotgun, a dainty twenty-gauge, that had remained with Nathan and his people.

Rahaita had been roused as well. She would recognize the sound of a firearm, and have reason to hate it — she had only seen the Krag used against her friends. No second report. It was double-barreled, so could have been fired again quickly. I wrapped a loincloth about me and stepped outside.

There were people rushing toward the house of Pua. Of course, that was where J.L. Nathan and his wife were lodged. Amelia too, and probably some of the others. Rahaita was beside me now and we hurried with the rest of the curious crowd. There was Heho on the porch, looking out at those who had gathered. Looking for me apparently, for he waved me to him.

"This is something you should see, Taona," he told me, as we entered the house. His eyes flickered to Rahaita at my side, acknowledged her, and went back to my face. "It is much like that which once happened to you in the house of the High King."

The assassination attempt? I followed him down the short hallway, to come upon a tableau in the central audience room.

There was James L. Nathan, holding the shotgun. On the floor, lay the young man we had seen earlier, quite dead. It was obvious to my eyes that his chest had received a shotgun blast at close quarters. The Mora gaping at his body knew nothing of such things.

Lady Pua crouched, examining the near-naked form by the torch light. "A priest, that is certain. You were right Rahaita," she said, glancing up at my wife. "And prepared for the rites of sacrifice. I fear I was intended to be that sacrifice.

"Does this seem familiar to you, Taona?" she asked, holding up a rose quartz knife. I remembered too well my encounter with a priestly assassin. This blade was a twin to the one he had carried. I only nodded.

"This snake came slithering in through our quarters, so I grabbed my girl here," Nathan said, holding up the gun, "and followed him. When he caught sight of me — should've been more careful — he pulled out the knife and rushed me. So I blasted him. Sort of out of reflex, but I am glad I did, my boy, or I might be the one lying here!"

"I am indebted to you, Neatanu," spoke Pua, rising to her feet. "Though I wish you had not made quite so large a hole in him. He might have been made to answer questions."

I looked over the body. Very young, no more than a boy, and very thin. He wore only a minimal breech-cloth and small ceremonial cap of bright feathers. Why would he wish to kill Pua? Was it a way to strike at the High King?

Assuming Pua was, indeed, his target — it seemed likely but who might know what had been in this dead boy's head?

"Your family is alright?" I asked James L. quietly, as the Mora busied themselves with removing the body.

"Oh, Judith never knew I got up. Probably realizes it by now. Amelia was spending the night with Demba, since young Watkins is off on his expedition to find clay. The two have become inseparable friends since we arrived."

"Gordie has done well by himself here."

"He's a good boy. His parents are friends — that's how he got to ship on the "Double Lucky" with a crew of more experienced sailors. Might have ended up an officer of the Nathan Line if our world hadn't gotten turned inside-out." He chuckled. "I'd best go and see if Judith woke up and missed me."

As James L. Nathan ambled down a side hall, shotgun tucked into the crook of his arm, I looked back at the room to see Rahaita in earnest conversation with Lady Pua. A moment later, the Mora noblewoman also slipped away and my wife came to me.

"Pua says she has much to speak about with you. She will call for you tomorrow." She stretched and grinned at me. "I am wide awake and very hungry. Do you think we could find some food?"

7. Priests

"We have known a priestly conspiracy has been growing for some time. The High Priest is not involved — he is an old fool who spouts the need for tradition, but would not upset what he has."

Pua and I were joined by Heho and Ma'are at this conference, which, of course, entailed a meal, spread on mats on her wide, high porch. From this vantage, one could keep an eye on most of the town. All of us seated ourselves in accordance with Mora protocol, Pua to my left, Heho to my right, his intended across from him. I gave Ma'are a good looking over and supposed she could be pregnant, but would not have sworn to it.

"Their leader calls himself Tahu," Heho informed me. The name would mean something like "the healed one" or maybe "healed by the gods."

"He has been harbored by Revaru," added Pua. "Revaru is not to be trusted."

"Nor Hara'a," murmured Ma'are. "We can't forget him."

I knew little of Hara'a, only that his realm was the most easterly of the nine Mora kingdoms, and that he had been the third, with Hei'iro and Revaru, to vote against Ve'eta as High King.

Pua slowly nodded. "The old ways are still followed in his corner of the land."

"What of Hei'iro?" I asked.

"Who can say? He is an honorable man but also a believer in the traditions others have discarded."

I considered this a moment or two, staring into my bowl of beer. "Revaru, then, might be less than honorable?" I asked.

"None of us would actually say that, Taona," Ma'are told me, but the knowing looks the three gave one another certainly implied it.

"It would be best not to pass through his lands on your way home," said Pua. "You could travel west into Anana's kindom, could you not?" she asked Heho.

"And follow the coast? We could but that is a very roundabout way to A'auwa, my lady." He shrugged. "But, yes, it would be safer. I even know a pass further west we could use, that opens into Anana's lands rather than those of Mahutunoa."

Lady Pua approved. "Mahutunoa is friendly to us, though some would call him weak. It might be just as well were you not spied passing through his kingdom."

"It is I who am the problem, as one of those who came from the sea — whether an hero or not. I know this," I told them. "None would have reason to harm Rahaita, would they?"

"She is the daughter of one who supports the High King," replied Pua. "That makes her an enemy in the eyes of some."

"Or at least someone who would attract interest," added Ma'are. "I do not think even the most fanatical followers of Tahu would attack the Lady Rahaita."

I was slightly amused that Ma'are and Heho referred to Rahaita as 'Lady.' Which is a poor approximation of the actual honorific but will have to do. No one had called her that in her father's home, but she was of a station that called for such a title, wasn't she? A princess. I was alright with it, as long as she didn't expect it of me.

"So when can we leave?" I asked.

Pua held up her hand. "Let us at least wait until the messengers return from Arierona." And from her son, as well, I would suspect. There would be many interested in us, for one reason or another. She looked at something going on below us. "Gordie has returned," she announced. "Go and speak with him, Heho."

As the half-Mora courier absented himself, the noblewoman took the opportunity to address Ma'are. "You two should wed before Heho runs off again. Who knows how long he might be gone this time?" I wondered why she would bring this up in front of me.

"We need a priest," objected Ma'are, rather weakly. Then she noted a smiling Pua's eyes were upon me. "You could do it, Taona!"

Oh, so that was how it went. "Rahaita and I were wed by the shaman Oorto. I am sure he is preferable. He is the real thing."

"Not in the eyes of our people, Taona Marareta," said Pua. "They have accepted you as a priest, whether you have or not."

I supposed I would have to get the proper tattoos, eventually. "If you truly think I would be acceptable, I would be honored," I told Ma'are. What Heho would think of our plotting, I knew not.

I had seen a Mora wedding once, that of my friends Poneiva and Beka to Rahaita's cousins in the house of Arierona. The rite was quite simple, as I remembered. I could probably handle it, with a little refresher as to the proper words.

"They found the dirt they sought," reported Heho on his return. He sat down and guzzled some beer, before continuing. "I should go and help them with it. Maybe later. I'm still hungry." He started in on one of the starchy pastes these people consumed in quantity. I could barely abide the stuff.

"The Taona has agreed to officiate your wedding ceremony," Pua informed him. "I think tomorrow evening would be a good time."

Heho choked on his mouthful of taro paste and had to wash it down with quite a quantity of beer. "Tomorrow?" he asked at last.

"I am assured it will be considered official if I preside," I told him.

"Why not?" he responded, and gulped more beer. "Now I suppose I'll have to fast the rest of the day."

"It is the custom," said Pua. "And you will need to keep away from Ma'are until tomorrow."

"I can manage. No different than being on the road." Heho looked fondly at his bride-to-be. "And a journey worth the taking."

8. Love

"Once Heho is wed, we can begin to make our way home."

"Home, Marareta?" Rahaita asked, her tone mocking. "Is my father's house to be our home?"

"It was by A'auwa that I met you, my wife. What better place is there for us to dwell in this world?"

"The lake is beautiful," she agreed, "but perhaps we should be on the shore opposite that house."

I felt that was not at all a bad idea. "I would think a messenger would come soon from your father." A man had already returned from the High King, reporting immediately and privately to Lady Pua. The news of our return was surely spreading among the Mora. Would Aranu's father, King Hei'iro, know of his safe return?

"Your father's men wish to return with us. All but Hito, who chooses to remain with Aranu."

"And perhaps vie with him for Amirea?" It was no secret both had been courting Miss Amelia Corrine Nathan. I favored neither; they were both good men. But I knew also there might be another.

"I wonder if Amirea harbors feelings for Bafa. I have heard they became close again while he recovered from his wounding."

Rahaita gave me a long and thoughtful look before she replied. Was she recalling that I, too, had once paid suit to Amelia? "She says he is as a brother to her. Whether I believe that, I am not sure."

I hoped it was so. Whatever the two might once have had, it belonged now to another world. We stood watching Dutch and his

Diwarna assistant work at the making of a potter's wheel. Their first design had proven flimsy and fallen apart; this one was heavier. Not too heavy for Amlee and Tala to use, I hoped.

It would be interesting to see what they crafted of the white clay they had brought back. Other deposits should be sought out, especially if they and their men decided to live in that empty valley we had passed through on our way from the mountains. Some of the half-caste men who had once followed Nesmith into those mountains were already returning there, and others with them. In a roundabout way, they had found the home he had promised them.

"That should do," said Dutch, giving the wheel a spin. "I've kept it simple," he told us. "Maybe I'll see about adding a foot treadle if I make another."

"The kick wheel should be perfectly good," I told him. "That was what they used across the mountains." I think I felt a little jealous of the two women right then, being able to settle into a creative trade. Maybe I could paint again some day.

"You will need to go back across those mountains some day and bring me some bronze tools," Dutch said. "Working with stone is mighty time-consuming."

"Could you not make some yourself?" asked Rahaita, having absolutely no idea what might be involved.

"Send your husband to find me some ore and I'll give it a try, Mrs. Malvern." My wife also had no idea what 'Mrs.' meant. She gave me a quizzical glance.

"'Wife of Marareta' that would be in our language," I explained. "It is customary among our people for a woman to be known by her husband's name."

She frowned. "That is a very bad custom, Marareta. It is good that you live among a more sensible people now."

To Dutch, I said, "It would be safer to call my wife Lady Rahaita.

"I'd best go prepare for this evening," I told Rahaita. "I don't want to make too many mistakes with my first wedding."

"You will use those funny signs you drew?" She was referring to the notes I had written out.

"Only if necessary. I was not trained to memorize things as readily as your people." A preliterate society, the Mora had a prodigious capacity for memorization. The couriers could quickly learn and recall quite long messages.

And I had found that young Ulani could recite thousands upon thousands of lines of epic poetry. Sometimes I felt I was the 'uncivilized' one here.

I noticed we were not heading toward our own little hut. "Where are we going?"

"Lady Pua has something for you," my wife responded.

That something proved to be priestly costuming. Had Pua made it herself? I did not know and felt it impolite to ask.

"This crown is the main thing," she told me. "That will mark you as a priest." It was a small peaked cap of feathers, not unlike what our would-be assassin had worn. These feathers were not so bright, however. I looked it over.

"Hawk feathers?"

"They were available, and suitable to one who is also a warrior." Pua held up a cape of bark cloth. The designs painted on it meant nothing to me. "We did not have enough feathers for a cloak but this will do."

"You should take the crown with you when we leave," Rahaita told me. "People will expect it." The cape would be too bulky and too fragile to carry with us.

I held the cap in my hands and gazed at it. "Do I wish to be one of these priests?" I mused, near-whispering. "Do I want to be like that boy who was slain here?"

"Priests come in good and bad, as do all men," replied Pua. "As for the assassin, he may have been only a lone fanatic, like the man who tried to kill you, Taona. But I fear otherwise."

"I suppose I have seen the worst of them," I said. "What god do I serve, anyway? Or a goddess, perhaps?"

"Like many wandering holy men, you are seen as serving all the gods," Rahaita told me.

"But you may certainly choose one as your patron, should you wish," added Lady Pua.

"The god of love," suggested Rahaita, "whose sign you wear." Then she snickered in a rather unladylike manner. I suppose she had recognized I was making that up of the whole cloth.

I didn't know if there even was a god of love. The only Mora deity I had heard much about was the Moon Goddess. Rahaita had chosen to rename me for the moon, calling me Marareta, 'Moon

King.' But Pana'a and her priestesses served that goddess. Not a good choice for me.

Pua nodded gravely. "Teva we name that god. He makes love to the earth by bringing the rain."

"Good enough." I put a finger to the small heart tattoo on my arm. "And this is an emblem of love, Rahaita, whether it is actually a leaf or not."

"Then I must indeed have one like it," said she.

9. Cliffs

The wedding went well and, fortunately, Teva sent no rain during the ceremony, nor during the feast that followed. My patron and I were off to a good start.

And after the things I had seen in the Valley of Visions, I was not certain but what the gods might be real. How much difference is there between a powerful wizard and a minor deity? But there was no time to spend thinking of such things. We must depart this place, journey to far Lake A'auwa, and see what awaited us.

For greater safety, a pair of traders chose to travel with us, Rahaita and I, Heho and a handful of Mora warriors. Moreover, they felt it might be good to know of this alternate pass of Heho's. We carried only what we could on our own backs, a pack basket for each of us.

I carried my wooden club, the one given me by Arierona, but in my pack was the bronze weapon I had ordered crafted in the Valley of Visions, carefully wrapped in a grass mat. I had other plans for it. A bronze knife now hung at my waist, and those of all the men who had crossed the mountains with me.

Of course, Heho could not be denied a day with his wife after the marriage ceremony, but early the next morning we set forth. I had seen another messenger arrive and closet with Pua the previous afternoon, but of what they spoke I did not learn. If it were something I truly needed to know, I trusted the noblewoman to inform me.

Rahaita sighed as we took to our road. "Did we not just finish walking?" she asked. There had been little enough rest since we had finished our long journey to this land. We followed the usual trade route only a few miles before Heho led us off into the trackless west.

"Better here, where the land is mostly flat, than closer to the hills," he explained. "We shall get enough of uneven ground, even so." I knew nothing of the area into which he led us, though I assumed there were Diwarna tribes there.

Over the next couple days, the savanna began to give way to a jungle of sorts. Not a rain forest; this was an ever thicker scrub and coarse head-high grasses, becoming harder to traverse. All the while, we angled toward the hills to our south. "It is worse to the north," said Heho. "No one could force his way through there."

Eventually, we began to climb into the hills, along the steep northern side of the range; to our right, the land had become marshy. "Beyond," said Heho, pointing westward, "lie the great mangrove swamps of the coast. Even here, there is salt in the water." Our way became an increasingly narrower strip of dry, rocky ground between the swampland and unbroken cliffs. That these cliffs were the same that bounded the Mora coastline I had little doubt. Further west would lie Ahurataca, the point that marked the northern edge of their homeland.

"If we go much further this way, we shall have to walk on the backs of crocodiles," complained one of the traders.

"No further," Heho replied. "There is our pass through the cliffs." He pointed to a broken area, choked with fallen rocks. "It is an easier way than it looks," he assured us.

The trader looked upward with a skeptical eye. "I can see why this path is little traveled," he remarked.

"No, it is not practical," agreed our guide. "But we who carry messages for the High King have long known we could go this way, if need arise." He started forward again, then stopped to warn us, "There are many scorpions here. Watch for them."

The climb was, indeed, not that bad, and none suffered the sting of a scorpion. We did see them, sunning themselves on the rocks, large and very dangerous looking. I have heard, though, the smaller varieties are more deadly. Having no real knowledge of such things, I will continue to avoid all of that tribe.

There was almost no hill on the far side, only a gradual sloping downward. "We are in the kingdom of Anana?" I asked Heho.

"We are. We can angle to the village of Marihana further along, if we wish. It lies just at the edge of Mahutunoa's lands, and we could take to canoes there. Or we could continue to travel south along the coast — all the way to Lake Aedina if we chose." He looked directly at me. It was my decision, apparently.

Va'aru, cousin of Hareata, ruled at Aedina and I knew him to be our friend. But it would make our journey to A'auwa much longer and perhaps no safer. "Marihana," I told him.

"Good," said a trader. "We left canoes at Marihana."

"And I am very tired of walking!" added Rahaita.

"I am sure my men are, too," I said, looking at the Mora warriors who had twice crossed the high mountains with me.

One of them, Rika, spoke in agreement. "That we are, Taona. But would it not be dangerous to be seen at this village?" Rika was always one who thought things through.

"Best you not show yourselves," said Heho. "We can pick you up a little downstream."

We continued south for a time, before turning more easterly. Days later, we saw the village of Marihana, jumping off point for most of the trade across the hills, nestled on a pebbly bank at a turn of the River Teiri. The name Marihana might translate as 'calm light' or maybe 'clear stillness' or something toward that concept. It did have that look to it as evening took us.

I would have liked to sit and talk with the traders there, learn the latest news of them, but I was far too recognizable. Best let Heho take care of that. I and Rahaita and our warriors camped a little further down the stream. It was not a very large river here, this tributary of the great Teoma, but broad and fairly shallow. Even this far up a few of the fish-eating crocodiles could be seen in its waters.

"Are we near the home of the High King here?" Rahaita whispered to me in the night, as we lay looking to the clear, star-filled skies.

"Fairly. We can turn aside to it or follow this river down to the Teoma. The shortest route to your father is through the High King's lands."

"I would rather not speak to Ve'eta."

"You know him?" That had never occurred to me.

"Yes. He has visited the houses of all the kings at one time or another. Ve'eta has campaigned to become High King all his life." I heard her giggle in the dark. "Or Lady Pua has campaigned, maybe!"

"He seemed to be a good young man." I had met him only briefly but the impression had been favorable.

"And very dull. He thinks only of fighting and food."

"Too much imagination is dangerous in kings," I told her.

"Ah, you are very wise, Taona. And I am very sleepy."

10. Power

"You need not fear meeting Ve'eta," Heho assured my wife. "He is not at his house right now, but with his uncle Temani'itu, at the coast." We had all fitted ourselves into three rather small canoes he and the two traders had brought down to us.

"Ah, then you can woo Panoha in peace," Rahaita told me.

"She, too, has departed, to dwell in the house of Hareata." Off to live with her brother. That must have been a let down after being a queen.

"Is *anyone* there?" I asked of him.

"Staff and retainers. Probably various cousins and other relatives — they come and go. That land over there," he gestured toward the left bank, "is the kingdom of Revaru. He will pay no attention to travelers on the river and we will soon be past it."

"Still, it would be just as well if no one knew we passed through the High King's lands," I felt.

"Agreed," said our guide. "With Ve'eta not in residence, there will be no insult to the High King's hospitality if we pass his house by."

My last journey on this river had been against the flow; sluggish it might be but it was still much more work than going this direction. Surprisingly soon, we reached the large, rounded, rust-colored rock on our left that marked the way to the High King's home. It also marked the end of Revaru's realm.

There was, as well, a very small village and a spot nearby where many left their vessels. Two canoes we dragged onto the bank and the traders departed in the third, with wishes of health and success going both ways. Then Rahaita looked about and stated, "This is a sacred place. I can feel it."

"Isn't that the Blood Stone?" asked Rika.

"Ah. Of course." I guess they knew what that meant. I had to ask Rahaita of it later, as we walked the well-marked road toward the house of Ve'eta.

"What is the Blood Stone?"

"I think the name is just because of its color, Marareta, though some claim one god or another bled there. But it is a place of power where dreams and visions sometimes come, even to those with no gifts." She turned her head to look at me. "As at the Place of the Crocodile that you visited with Oorto."

"How can a place have power? I understand the power you or Oorto or Hurasu holds. That is in your minds."

"You spoke with Hurasu of the gates between worlds, did you not?" I nodded an assent. "He told me gateways may lie all about us, unseen and unopened. Gates that can *not* be opened, unlike the ones through which you and he passed into this world." She gathered her thoughts. "Yet they are, um, not completely closed, maybe. And things come through or we partially pass through. Or something. People do see things at such places. They do have meaningful dreams. That is probably enough to know."

So she said nothing more and I asked nothing more. Both of us probably understood it about as well as we ever would. I wondered, however, if the Sacred Island of Pana'a was also such a place of power. If it were, sitting there so close to the house of Arierona, it was no wonder that it might have driven Rahaita's mother to madness.

There is little to tell of that long walk across Ve'eta's realm and into that of Arierona. We passed east of the house of the High King and then took to the road Heho and I had once traveled, through the low hills that separated the two lands, and down to A'auwa, avoiding villages as much as was possible. Not that we really needed to hide our identities by this point. It would not hurt for Arierona to know we were coming.

It remained a land of great beauty, not as lush here as further west, but still fruitful. Much of the ancient forest yet stood, here and there, among the cultivated fields. We crossed many streams, rushing to join Teoma by one route or another, and there were fishes in those streams, and birds in the trees beside them.

At last, we stood on the shore of A'auwa and gazed across its waters at the house of Arierona. "We could wait for the raft to come and ferry us across," said Heho. He looked up at the sun. "It would be a long wait and we may be too many for one load."

"We can cross at the upper end," suggested Rahaita. "I can walk a little further."

I had never seen the head of the lake, but everyone nodded agreement so I decided it must be a good idea. There was a well-traveled pathway, leading along an increasingly heavily wooded shore. We passed at least two secluded shrines to one deity or another as the morning passed into afternoon.

Where the Teoma flowed into A'auwa between high banks, we came to a suspension bridge. Made of the same strong rope, I noted, as used on the coastal cliffs. "It is years since I crossed here," said Rahaita. "I and my cousins used to come and explore. This is where they first met Poneiva and Maneata." She laughed. "Then they just wanted to explore them!"

It would be good to see Poneiva; Maneata, alas, had passed to wherever Mora heroes rested. But Beka — onetime sailor Bobby Beck — had become a new brother to Poneiva, and even married Maneata's fiancee. E'eva and Miruhata, their wives, Rahaita's cousins, would also be a welcome sight. Particularly so if they were caring for the son I had not yet met.

We filed quietly along the shore toward the house of Arierona, as dusk began to fall upon the lake. This was home for most of us; even for me. Heho was at home everywhere, I suppose. I could catch a glimpse now of Arierona's high roof, its thatch burnished by the setting sun.

And there, waiting for us by the docks, stood Pana'a. Rahaita ran to embrace her.

"Did you see that we were coming?" she asked.

"No, my silly girl," replied her aunt. "Messengers told your father and he told me. It is much quicker for a canoe to cross A'auwa with news than it is for you to walk all the way around!

"But come. There is a father who awaits his beloved daughter." She turned to me. "And there is a father who must meet his son."

11. Children

King Arierona stood before his house. He did not wear his high feathered crown nor did he hold his heavy obsidian-headed spear.

But he held his daughter in his arms and he wept. "I thought you lost forever, my child." And then, most uncharacteristically for that very formal man, he sat down there on the steps with Rahaita at his side, and looked at me.

"It is you, Marareta, that I must thank for this. I think no other man might have brought Rahaita back to me."

I took this opportunity to remove the covering from my bronze sword-club and present it to the king. "Once you gave me a club to use in battle. Now I bring one to you from beyond the mountains."

"It was enough, Hero from the Sea, that you returned my daughter to me." He turned to the young man who stood near by. "Perhaps you should carry this, my son."

George Bath picked up the weapon and grinned. "Far too heavy for me, sir. I am not going to grow any larger!"

Arierona took it back from him. He tested the edge with his thumb and raised an eyebrow at the unexpected sharpness. "Of what is this made? No, we can speak of such things later. We must feast! All must rejoice with me. But you," he said, "will wish to see your own child." He stood and looked toward Pana'a, before announcing to those gathered, "We shall celebrate tomorrow. All day and as much of the night as we are able!"

Rahaita whispered into his ear. "Of course, my dear," he replied softly. "But return soon."

HERO FROM THE SEA

She slipped to my own side and said, "Let's go meet your son." We followed Pana'a into the house, Arierona stepping aside to let us pass first, in a gesture of hospitality.

I remembered where Pana'a's room lay, but we headed elsewhere. Rahaita's quarters, I believed, had been somewhere in the direction we went. I had never had reason to visit those when I resided here before. As we entered a room, much like any other room in this house though larger than most, E'eva squealed and ran to embrace Rahaita. The more reserved Miruhata was able to restrain herself for a few moments. Smiling indulgently at the trio, Pana'a took me by the arm. "Over here."

How old would this little boy who lay sleeping, oblivious to the excitement, be? Three months, perhaps? I would have to count back to — oh, it didn't matter.

Pua was right. He was a handsome child. Black was his hair, as black as that of his mother. Would those eyes, once opened to see his father's face, be as dark and piercing as hers? Or would they be as my own, shifting with the light? The three girls gathered around us now and I, as had Arierona, wept as I took my child into my arms.

When we laid him back down to sleep, I embraced each of those girls, the young women who had cared for my son, as well. "Our husbands are out with Ponu, patrolling along the border," Miruhata told me. "They will want to see you as soon as they return."

"As I would wish to see them. Too bad they will miss the party."

"Messengers have been sent. They might make it back in time," said E'eva. "Now what is this about you marrying our Rahaita?"

"Oh, I have decided to take Panoha as my wife instead," I announced. Well, I thought it was funny, even if they didn't. As we told the pair our tale, Pana'a slipped away unnoticed. This must, on some level, be painful for her, I with another beside me, our child whom she must entrust to the care of others.

It would be dark out by now. Had those who accompanied us been cared for, found quarters? "I should check on Heho and the others," I told Rahaita. "Will you join me for a meal later?" She nodded somewhat absently and turned her attention back to her friends.

I wandered out into the gardens. Heho, I knew, would have no problem fending for himself. The warriors might be a bit lost after their long absence. Ah, there was Rika.

He greeted me as I approached. "Taona. This is my wife Hepetea," he said, and kissed the woman his arm was wrapped around. "It is very good to be home!"

No problems for Rika, then. "Have the others found their places here?"

"Oh, yes. We are all happy. Even Heho." He looked about as if trying to locate the courier. "I think he is looking for a second wife!" That sounded about right. "Taona?"

"Yes, Rika?"

"If you need warriors of your own — um, I would serve you." He looked at his wife as if seeking her approval but I don't think she was taking him too seriously. Rika had consumed a fair amount of beer, obviously.

"I am only a poor priest, Rika. But I shall keep it in mind." That seemed to satisfy both of them. I wandered down to the shores of A'auwa, as once I had many a night. A light breeze rippled the surface of the lake, lit by a piece of moon and the many stars.

"I expected you to find your way down here eventually," said Pana'a, who sat in the grass, gazing out. I took a place beside her.

"What are we to name our son?" she asked.

"I had considered Maneata," I said. Maneata, for the man who had befriended me when I was a stranger in this world, the man who had given his life for my people, the man who was brother to my friends Poneiva and Beka. "But I think now it might be better to save that name."

"I would agree with this."

"He is a child of the moonlight," I said. "Born of the priestess of the moon."

"And of the Moon King," said she. "What think you of Maratoa?"

Maratoa, the Moon Warrior. "It is a good name. Let us make it so."

I could see her nod agreement in the dim light. "Before I became Pana'a, I was know as Rahiri. It is a name I was told to forget but I am Rahiri and Rahiri is me, always." Pana'a turned toward me and continued, "If you have a girl, will you name her for me?"

"I will," I promised. Rahaita would certainly approve of that.

Rahaita. I should go and see if she waited for me on the veranda of Arierona, ready to share a meal before we retired. I rose. "Farewell, Pana'a."

"Farewell, Hero from the Sea."

12. Feasting

We did indeed feast all day and most managed the night, as well. I sat at the right hand of Arierona, Rahaita at his left, at the formal feast, and also later when there was time for us to talk. The story of our adventures was a long one.

And we did tell him of our marriage. No, the king did not consider it valid in Mora society, nor did he suggest we make it so anytime soon. But he said nothing against our union, and that was for the good. Arierona certainly knew we shared a sleeping chamber.

I had told Rahaita the previous evening, as we had taken a late supper, of the name chosen for my son. She thought it a good one, and after eating we went immediately to the baby and informed him as well. He did not object.

Arierona thought it a fine name, too. "Will you adopt the child as your own?" he asked, and then immediately realized we would have to be married for that. That, also, we took as a good sign, and ignored the king's momentary embarrassment.

Those who had followed me over the mountains, warriors of Arierona, were honored as well and sat arrayed to my right. But there was much more to that celebration than sitting and eating.

Eat we did, however, of roast pig and ducks, and of fish taken from the lake. I remembered how Bath had once spent his days angling for those fish; his place has risen greatly here, as high as it was possible. The many types of fruit grown or gathered in this land were in great heaps for the taking. All the varieties of taro paste were available in carved wooden bowls, and yams and all the millet beer one might desire.

Many groups of feasters were spread across the king's porch and his garden, and many wandered between these groups to listen to storytellers or watch dancers or to merely gossip with others who had gathered here. Leaving Rahaita with her cousins a while, I wandered myself, coming upon Heho. The lean courier was sitting quietly beneath a spreading hibiscus, watching people come and go, and sipping beer.

"Your friends have made it here," he said, and pointed. Looking across the crowded garden, I saw Beka and Poneiva. At the moment, they were engaged by their parents, and their little sister Teme, as well. I could greet them later.

I sat beside Heho and helped him watch the crowd for a minute or two. "How long do you remain here, my friend?" I asked him.

"I know not," he replied, and paused to appreciate a young woman walking by. "Lord Hareata is coming soon. I shall see if he needs me." It did not surprise me to hear that Hareata would be on his way.

I could see Beka and Poneiva's wives had joined them, and Rahaita with them. "I should go speak with them," I told Heho, "though I think I could readily fall asleep here for a while."

"That would not do for the hero of the day. Arierona expects you to be seen." The courier spoke lightly but, of course, he was right. I rose to go greet my old friends. "I shall see you again, Heho," I told him. "Behave yourself with the women until then."

"Me, Taona? I am a married man, as you well know. That as-sumes," he added with a grin, "your ceremony was valid."

It was as though I had left the brothers yesterday. As a result, we did not have that much to say to each other. Some friends are like that, there for presence more than conversation. In time, they wandered away with their wives to greet other friends, and Rahaita disappeared somewhere too, and I found myself standing with Teme.

Teme had grown considerably since last I saw her. Girls do that at her age and it was likely she would not grow much more. At least not in height. She was as lean and angular as ever, and just as self-possessed. "I hope you do not mind too much that I have tak-en another as wife," I said, recalling our agreement — not intended too seriously by either of us — to marry in a few years if neither found someone else.

"Oh, no, Taona, I don't care about that anymore. I intend to marry Bafa!"

At least he was closer to her own age. Let me see, she must be fifteen and he was, what, somewhere in his early-to-mid twenties? I was finding it more and more difficult to keep track of such things in this equatorial land where one did not note the passage of the seasons. Anyway, it was a smaller difference than that between Ra-haita and myself. In two or three more years, it might be consid-ered a perfectly good match.

I know such differences are rarely a good thing, and I have told that I resisted the idea of us being together. Rahaita had a maturity that is unusual. Perhaps Teme did, too. She was certainly every bit as headstrong.

"And does Bafa have anything to say about this?" I asked.

She scowled. "He hasn't noticed me yet. But he will!"

And who might stroll up to us at that moment but George Bath himself? "Ah, my prize student," he said in greeting to Teme. To me, he confided, "Teme is quite good with the bow. One of our best shots."

Teme glowed. So he had noticed her. Maybe not in the way she hoped, but I'm sure the girl felt it was a start.

"You've been teaching archery?" I asked him.

"That I have. We have a good corps of halfway decent bowmen now. I had to teach them the three-finger grip. It seems the Kohari use a pinch technique and those Mora who had any experience had picked that up."

That was all somewhat uninteresting to me, but each man has his passions. Maybe each fifteen year old girl, too.

Fifteen. Mora, as a rule, did not marry early. Rahaita must have turned twenty one by the time we were wed and that was not at all unusual. Young people were not expected to settle down too soon. On the other hand, they were not expected to wait as long as had I!

"I should find Rahaita," I told the two, and each of us went a different direction.

I did find my wife, seated by her father, the two of them quietly conversing. I joined them without speaking and sat, doing no more than watching her and knowing how fortunate a man I was.

A man who had lost a world so he might win something much greater.

It was inevitable that Arierona would eventually wish to speak with me in private. "I shall be by A'auwa when the sun rises," he whispered to me later, perhaps not wishing his daughter to hear. "Come to me then." No sleeping in for me, apparently. No sleeping at all, maybe.

13. Prophecies

As I reached the lake, in the gray just before dawn, I saw a canoe disappearing into the mists. Pana'a? She had not shown at the feast. Perhaps the priestess had been with our son.

The king soon joined me, coming down from his house with a pair of attendants. They stood at a discreet distance as we gazed out over A'auwa and spoke. "I will not disagree, Marareta, that you are an hero and deserving of my daughter," said Arierona. "I can not disagree. But I do not believe this is best for her or for her people."

"These are things I long told myself, my Lord Arierona, that I was not important enough, powerful enough, young enough. I came like a beggar to your door, depending upon your kindness. Yet, Rahaita has chosen. And I chose too, chose to follow her across the mountains, chose to bring her back to you, chose to love her."

The king listened to this and perhaps even grudgingly approved of it. There was a trace of resignation in his voice when he spoke again. "It could be said an alliance with an hero of prophecy is a good thing too. If you are that hero."

"I would rather give Bafa the privilege."

"And he would rather you take it on. Two very reluctant heroes you are! Ah, well, the gods will sort it out. It was prophesied and here you are."

"My lord —" I was uncertain of how I wanted to say this. "You must know your daughter is a prophetess as well."

"Yes, that was not hidden in the tale you have told me." He looked out toward the island of the priestesses, barely visible in the dim light. "We are still some days from the full moon. We will ask Pana'a to seek a new prophecy then."

"There is no surety there will be any foretelling." I knew that prophecy came when it would.

"No, there is not. Hareata intends to come to us for it, anyway." So that was why he was on his way. And had not Pua told me they would seek this?

"Rahaita tells me that is the mark of Teva on your arm."

I could not help smiling, perhaps a bit foolishly, at that. "Men do not know of Teva where I was born, Lord Arierona, but this is the sign of Cupid, who is like him in some ways."

"Are not the same gods everywhere?"

"I do not know. Perhaps they are, but with different names." They all came from our own human needs, did they not? Those were the same in all worlds.

"You should have the emblems of Teva on you, if you serve him. But I ask you not have yourself marked as the husband of Rahaita. Not yet."

I hadn't particularly planned to get any tattoos, so I was willing to agree to this. I nodded without speaking.

"Where do you journey now, Taona?" asked the king. "I do not think you will abide long in my house. Even with Rahaita here."

Was that so? I did feel I had duties yet but what they were, exactly, I was not sure. I had finished one great task, the returning of his daughter to Arierona. Or maybe the true task had been the winning of Rahaita for myself and her father was incidental to that. Surely I could rest for a time?

"Perhaps we will know better what the future holds for all of us after the full moon," I answered.

Arierona chuckled. "Spoken like a politician, Mareata. Or like a priest. We both should find our beds now." He turned without further word toward his high house.

There were more than a few from the feast stretched here on the grass, sleeping it off. I had done just that in this spot on occasion, but there was a wife waiting for me now in that house. I followed the king.

It was not until afternoon that I roused. I had sensed that Rahaita had risen some time earlier and left me, but I had quickly fallen back into sleep. As I lay there, yet half-awake, I heard her voice, and those of Miruhata and E'eva from the next room.

And another. Who? I groped about for my loincloth. It smelled of beer — must have spilled some on it last night — but I wrapped it around my waist and went to the doorway. Ah, it was Teme with them.

"Maratoa is very handsome," the girl told me. "Bafa and I will have many handsome sons!"

It was with some effort I kept a straight face. "Have you chosen names for them?" I asked.

"Of course not, Taona. That would be silly."

"I suppose it would," I admitted, but I suspected Teme might be pulling my leg. I smiled and shook my head at the girl. "How do Poneiva and Beka put up with you?"

"They send her home to her parents," said E'eva. "I think they only married us to escape this one."

"Undoubtedly," agreed Miruhata. "Let's go find those husbands of ours." A moment later, Rahaita and I were alone with my son. Our son? We were going to adopt him as such, once we were formally wed by Mora custom, weren't we? When that might happen, I did not know.

The boy was fussing. Rahaita picked him up and rocked him in her arms. Who was nursing the baby? Surely not Pana'a; she was not here enough for that.

My wife looked up from the baby she held. "I do wonder why Pana'a allowed herself to become pregnant," she said.

Mora women knew something of how to prevent conception, when they might be fertile and when they might not. There were several taboos connected to this knowledge. Pana'a had chosen to have a child with me. Had she seen some future for our son, some need?

"Only your aunt would know that." Unless Rahaita chose to seek into the future herself. That I would not suggest.

"Perhaps," she suggested, putting the pacified child back into his crib. "I too should allow myself to become pregnant."

"I am always willing to give it a try," was my answer.

14. Adoptions

"I spoke with Oorto," Rahaita quietly told me. "It was the first time we have attempted it on this side of the mountains."

I had never doubted the time would come that these two would again test their powers. "Is he well?"

She nodded. "It seems so, though something troubles his heart. Things go smoothly at the village."

The only thing that might trouble Oorto's heart, I was fairly sure, would be his beloved Ulani. A plump woman entered the room, holding a child. "Ah, here is Miri. We can leave Maratoa in her care now."

I had learned there was a wet-nurse for Maratoa, two of them, in fact. Of his mother, I saw nothing, but was told she was preparing for the rites of the full moon. That was but three days away now.

As we wound through the hallways of Arierona's house, I asked, "Then Oorto is still at the trade village?"

"He is. He says he made a quick trip home and then returned."

"I wonder if there is a large pile of earthen pots now. If Amlee and Tala have been successful, we might see such wares find their way even to here."

"If they were brought by the route we followed, they would arrive in many pieces." We stepped out onto the porch. There was always food to be found there, at any time of day or night.

This morning, something different was to be found. "Lord Hareata!"

HERO FROM THE SEA

The bulky Mora nobleman looked up. He had been conferring with, not surprisingly, Heho. "Taona," he greeted me. "Lady Rahaita. Join us."

Heho moved over to make a space between himself and Hareata, as I most definitely outranked him. Rahaita took a place across from us. "It has been long, Marareta. I hear you have become a great hero." He gave Rahaita a sidelong look. "And perhaps a husband?"

"Most definitely a husband," stated my wife.

"As is your father, I am not certain this should be," said Hareata. "I will not conceal this. We had hopes that you would wed Ve'eta."

"And that my Marareta would marry your sister. Yes, Lord Hareata, I know this." She licked some taro paste from her finger. "Many things that are hoped for do not come to be."

Heho's face remained impassive but he surreptitiously nudged me in the ribs. He was very much on my Rahaita's side in this exchange.

"Maybe we should introduce Bafa to the Lady Panoha," I suggested. "He is at least as heroic as I am."

"You jest with me, Taona, but the point is taken. One hero indeed might do as well as another."

Rahaita could not help laughing. "What would that do to poor Teme?"

That had to be explained to Hareata, who did not seem overly surprised. "In truth, that would not be a bad match. It is far too soon to plan such things, however." To me, he said, "I must tell you Panoha does not disfavor the idea of a match with you. You made a good impression at the house of Maitoa. I speak only the truth of this and will now say no more."

That somewhat took the fun out of the situation. And though Hareata intended to say no more *now*, I was sure the subject would pop up again.

"Have you been with my father, my lord?" asked Rahaita.

"We only came from him," was the reply. "Not that there was much to discuss. We shall await the full moon and the foretellings of Pana'a."

He turned again to me. "I must see this son of yours."

"He is a beautiful child," averred Rahaita. "He has the sea-colored eyes of his father."

"Maratoa, correct?" We both nodded. "Your cousin, Rahaita."

"But we shall make him our son," she replied.

"Hmm. Yes, you might do that. You might, indeed. That reminds me," he continued, "Pua sent a message that she has officially adopted that young storyteller of hers. Without her brother to forbid it, there was no stopping her."

"Ulani," I said. This would let the boy travel more readily into the land of the Mora and practice the craft of the storyteller, no longer without caste. No wonder Oorto felt concern.

Rahaita giggled. "Brother to the High King? What will Ve'eta think of that?"

"Oh," responded Hareata with a broad smile, "that boy learned long ago not to cross his mother."

15. A Full Moon

Beneath a full moon, we stood on the shore of A'auwa, waiting for a prophecy. We watched a canoe slowly approach, one erect dark figure paddling toward us. That figure silently pulled her canoe onto the sand and turned to approach us.

The prophecy was not to be delivered by Pana'a herself — who rested after her effort — but was recited to us by the one of the older priestesses.

From an ancient house one journeys,
to bring all the land together;
to give all the land its king
comes the hero from the sea.

Having spoken, the gray haired woman returned to her canoe and paddled back to the Sacred Island.

We all stood thinking on these words for a few moments.

"Then the hero will become High King?" wondered Arierona.

Hareata shook his head. "It does not say that. One must take care with prophecies."

"But it *could* mean that," I pointed out.

"Yes. Or it could mean quite the opposite and the hero will help Ve'eta reestablish his authority."

Arierona spoke again, the words coming slowly. "Somehow, I doubt that."

"As do I," said Hareata, "but I shall assume nothing."

The fourth of us standing there, Bafa — George Bath — broke his silence. "We should have had Beka here. He is better material for this promised hero from the sea." Bobby Beck was certainly more heroic in appearance and had distinguished himself as a fighter, but seemed content with his role as a follower of others.

"It would not hurt to keep him and his brother close," felt Hareata. "They could accompany me on my return to the High King." He looked then at me. "As should you, Taona."

"Should I? For what purpose?" I had no desire to leave Rahaita and the shores of A'auwa.

"For many reasons," Hareata said. "Hei'iro is there and will want to speak to you of his son. The High King will wish to know more of those who came from the sea. You might advise me, for I do value your voice." I suspected he also wished me in the vicinity of his sister. None of these reasons, neither on their own nor together, was enough. I am certain my face showed this.

"I wish it," said Arierona. "I wish you to go as my envoy, to defend my house."

I pondered that for only a moment, before inclining my head to the king. "For that reason, Lord Arierona, I am willing to go."

To defend his house, yes, for Rahaita and I were a part of that house. Admittedly, I also desired that the king would look favorably upon me and my marriage to his daughter.

And then, there was this prophecy. Did I have a role to play in what would come in this land? Or did it speak of another? I might as well find out.

Heho, who had stood well back, partway between us and a handful of attendants, stepped forward now. "You must be as weary of traveling as I am, Taona, but here we shall once more take the road together." He addressed Hareata. "How soon, my lord?"

"There is no hurry." The nobleman glanced at Arierona to see if he might have any opinion about that. "Three days. Now I must send messengers before I may sleep." He turned and walked up the slope toward the king's house. We followed.

"I would I journeyed with you," said Rahaita, when I told her of this, "as I have before. But I know that would not be wise."

"Nor would it be kind to take you again from your father so soon," I told her. "We have three days. Let us make the most of them."

Those days passed far too quickly, and I must give attention — at least from time to time — to things other than loving my wife. Plans were laid, farewells were made, not the least of these to Pana'a who came to the house of Arierona on the last day.

And before leaving that house, I did find the artist of the tattoo needle — which, here, was a sliver of sharpened bone — and had her add a second heart beside the one on my arm. That would be enough for now.

Part II. Kings

16. The Teoma

I did hold Rika to his promise to serve me. Arierona was entirely willing to let the warrior accompany us.

Beka also came. Poneiva, however, remained behind. I could see no reason for both brothers to come and neither could anyone else, truly. I charged the man to keep an eye on my wife and son while I was gone. None would I trust more than Poneiva, who was not only a fine warrior but also a man with brains. He would be a leader of men, in time.

We trekked north along the shores of A'auwa, past the falls known also as Pana'a, and paralleled the River Teoma. Along with my modest entourage of two, Hareata led half a dozen warriors, plus, of course, Heho.

"I shall leave our party in a couple days," the courier informed me. "Hareata has messages for me to bear to Lady Pua."

"Be sure to give your wife my greetings."

"I shall, Taona. Never did I think I would someday long to be with a wife rather than free and traveling the roads. Yet I miss Ma'are greatly." He grinned at me. "Having a wife is a very good thing, is it not?"

"I wouldn't have married the two of you if I thought otherwise."

Below the last fall on the Teoma — until one nearly reached the coast — we took to canoes. It was here we parted with Heho, who crossed the river and disappeared from our view.

I shared a canoe with Hareata, so we might converse on our journey toward Lake Aedina. With Heho gone, there was none other who could speak knowledgeably of the political situation. Nor of much else.

"The house of Arierona," he said to me, "could well be the 'ancient house' of the prophecy. It is the oldest of all the Mora dynasties."

"Either Bafa or I could be said to come from it, physically. Not in an hereditary sense, though."

"But Bafa was adopted by Arierona."

"Oh. Yes, that is true." I hadn't thought of that, for some reason. The very idea of that former fop now being the heroic son of a king was hard to take seriously. He seemed much the same fellow as always.

We lazily paddled along. Here, the flow of the Teoma could do most of the work and we need only steer, should we wish. As we passed further down the river we entered the most populous part of the Mora homeland, the kingdoms of Avatu and Va'aru. It was also the area, I had been told, where traditional customs and taboos were least likely to be observed.

Later, as our conversation came back around to politics, Lord Hareata said, "Understand, Marareta, I have no personal loyalty to Ve'eta nor to his mother. I support them as the best choice for our people.

"If nets had been cast wide enough, there are scores of men who might have been named as High King. Even our friend Poneiva."

"Poneiva?" That was news to me.

"His mother would be a second cousin to Lady Pua. That is somewhat distant but not too much to disqualify him."

I remembered what Amapa, Poneiva's father, had told me: "All the noble families are connected in some degree." A sudden thought made me smile. "Then the son of Teme could be High King?"

The big man chuckled. "I suppose he could."

After a few days, we passed by the mouth of the Teiri, the river that flowed past Marihana. Canoes carried much trade up and down its length, as they did the Teoma.

"Is our destination the house of Va'aru?" I asked.

"Not at once," was Hareata's unsatisfying reply. If not the house of his cousin, the king, then where?

"But the High King is there?"

"He is. You might do well not to go rushing to Ve'eta." There would be good reasons for that, I was sure, but Hareata did not seem to want to share them right then.

Before reaching the waters of Aedina, we turned our canoes to a village on our left, the southern shore of the river. The people there seemed to know Lord Hareata well and were rather nonchalant about the presence of a great noble. "My house lies a short distance from the river," he told us. We followed a shaded path; a small stream sang beside us. There were groves of bananas and papayas and some sort of citrus.

73

HERO FROM THE SEA

"I would have expected Hareata to have a bigger place," mused Beka, as we finally saw it rising before us. The sprawling home of his adoptive parents was certainly quite a bit larger. This was perhaps no roomier than the house in which Pua dwelt and did business at the trade village. But it had a bit of the look of a fortress to it, and sat atop a low hill.

One of Hareata's warriors heard him. "This house was built in the old days, when civil war ravished the nation, before the first High King was chosen," he informed us. "Once, a palisade stood about it but that is forbidden now." It would be very old then, as old, perhaps, as Arierona's house. That too, it occurred to me, was set on a hill.

"Ah," said Hareata, "Temani'itu is here."

17. The House of Hareata

I had briefly met Temani'itu when he took his fleet north to rescue my friends from the Kohari. I could not say I knew him well, or at all, for that matter. He looked much like his brother, the late High King Maitoa. Like that brother, he was a bulky man, with a craggy face and heavy brow.

Nor was he young. I would doubt Temani'itu was inclined to travel much by land in a world where the only choices were a litter or ones own legs.

"He has a house in the lands of the High King but rarely goes there," Hareata confided to me. "Temani'itu does not like to be far from the sea."

The old admiral — I know of no better title for him — sat drinking beer on the steps before Hareata's house. Two women sat with him, one of whom I recognized as Panoha. I wondered if the other might be Hareata's wife.

"Lord Hareata," the man rumbled, and held up a huge hand in greeting. "I thank you for the hospitality of your house. Even if I did help myself!"

"You are always welcome here, Lord Temani'itu," replied Hareata. Formalities out of the way, he sat down next to his guest and asked, "How do you, Temmi?"

I tried to follow their chatting, which seemed to hold nothing of importance, but all the while I felt the eyes of Panoha upon me. Did she think I had come here for her?

And, even worse, did Hareata plan it that way?

HERO FROM THE SEA

Lord Hareata's servants saw to it I was squared away and installed in a rather small windowless room. In that the walls of these Mora houses are mostly grass mats, ventilation is not such a great concern — and one can always go sleep on a porch if ones room is too stuffy. Then I joined him and his guest for an evening meal. There were only the three of us, the men, that is, so I had no difficulty recognizing that I should take the lowest place.

"This is my wife, Mehetu," Hareata said, indicating the tall woman directly to his left. "Panoha, you know."

"My Lady Mehetu. Lady Panoha," I acknowledged them. I would commit to no more than formalities. Apparently, the nobleman had but one wife. As much as he traveled, even one was likely to be neglected.

We ate a while in silence before talk began, inevitably, of politics. "Hei'iro may join us. I do not know," Temani'itu was saying.

"He certainly shares our concerns."

Temani'itu nodded. "We may have your friend from the sea to thank for making him more well disposed toward us." He turned in my direction. "Having his son return from across the mountains has certainly put Hei'iro in a better mood."

"And return as an hero," added Hereata. "Perhaps he should have come all the way home but I understand why he did not." The Mora smiled. "I hear now he may return with a wife."

This was certainly the first I had heard of it. "Amirea, my lord?"

"Indeed. Lady Pua tells us she has accepted his suit."

"That is the girl we rescued? Pale little thing."

Hareata laughed well at that. "She has darkened up nicely with some sun, Temmi. And she is a bit of a warrior, I hear, and deadly with a bow."

She was, wasn't she? Maybe she and Aranu would make a good match, and have many obstreperous children.

"We should speak of marriages," Hareata continued. "Your marriage, Taona." Oh, no, not in front of Panoha!

"A marriage between you and the daughter of Arierona makes Ve'eta and his advisers suspicious. He does not have good advisers now, having sent his mother away and not listening to his uncle." His eyes went to Temani'itu and then back to me. "They whisper to him that you have designs on his throne, or that Arierona does."

This was more complicated, then, than I had known. I thought the High King simply wanted Rahaita, not that he feared conspiracies. I saw also, though it might not have been intended, that these men, yes, and Lady Pua, wanted to control the young High King. There was no need for me to help them with that.

"We would like to see a joining of the House of Arierona to that of the High King," admitted Hareata. "There is no need to hide that fact. Both you and Rahaita need to consider what is best for all." He did not sound like he believed that would make me reconsider.

And it wouldn't. I'd best not mention that Arierona did not seem all that set against our marriage. Indeed, the king's remarks had sounded just a tad like that conspiracy he had mentioned.

"In the mean time," he continued, "there is growing unrest, fanned by fanatical priests. Something needs to be done."

Temani'itu belched and shrugged. "If the people have the things they need and are not mistreated, there is no unrest. The priests fan a flame from embers that already smoldered."

The admiral was a realist. As such, his voice would probably be ignored.

"I would fan a flame in some tobacco leaves," said Hareata. "Shall we go to the porch and smoke?" Leaving the women behind without so much as word, the two ambled away. I chose to acknowledge the ladies before following, having been brought up to be polite.

"You do not smoke, do you, Marareta?" asked Hareata, as the two filled large bamboo pipes. There was most certainly *kalina*, hemp leaf, mixed with that tobacco.

"I do not, my lords. But this will do," I said, as I accepted another bowl of beer from one of the servers.

"We shall travel on to the house of Va'aru in a day or two," said my host. "Enjoy my hospitality until then. And," he continued, "know Panoha would not object to being a second wife. Think upon it."

"Not until my marriage to Rahaita is recognized," I told him. This I thought he understood, that I would not even consider the subject until then. Later I wondered if he thought I meant it as a promise to marry Panoha once I had Rahaita as my lawful wife.

Either way, that was sometime in the future and I would not worry about it now. It was many bowls of beer later I stumbled to my room and my sleeping pad. I feared for a moment that Mehetu or Panoha or both might come to my room and offer to stay, as a gesture of hospitality. But it did not happen and soon I slept.

18. By Aedina

Hareata held up a hand to attract the attention of one of his attendants and then pointed to his head. In a few seconds, the man brought him a feather crown. "I should wear this to greet Ve'eta," he told me.

"Should I put mine on too?" I asked.

"Certainly." He seemed amused.

I rummaged in my basket and found the cap. Before I could place it on my head, the nobleman held out his hand. "May I?" I handed it to him.

He turned it over a couple times, nodded, and handed it back. "It is fitting, I think."

I slipped it on. Hareata's was only of moderate height, and predominantly of blue and green. If there was a significance to the color of the feathers — or the birds from which they came — I did not know.

We had dallied a day and the better part of another at Hareata's home before boarding our canoes and venturing onto Lake Aedina. There, on its shores, lay the high house of Va'aru, and in that house waited not only the kings Va'aru and Hei'iro but the High King Ve'eta as well.

And, while idling at his house, did I speak with Hareata's sister and even allow the Lady Panoha to flirt some with me? That I did; it cost me nothing and time spent with her was pleasant enough. At least, I am sure I offended no one.

I would be more concerned about that here. Mora protocol was tricky, the more so since there were religion-based taboos interwoven through it. The less I did to call attention to myself, the better. I followed Hareata into the great central room.

Va'aru I recognized, standing at Ve'eta's right. Much like Hareata was he, similar in size, build, even face; but Hareata had a vitality about him his cousin could not match. I knew the man to be capable of feats of athleticism that belied his size.

And that must be Hei'iro, slightly behind our host. Short, fat — there was little resemblance to his large and powerful son, Aranu. His face was round, his eyes in something of a perpetual squint. I knew not if I would find opportunity to speak to him today, but he would want to know of his son.

Then there was the High King himself, Ve'eta, looking like a very overgrown boy. He conversed at some length with Hareata before turning his attention to me.

"I remember you, Taona!" He placed his right hand on my left shoulder in greeting, and I reciprocated. This was the greeting of equal to equal, an honor — an honor his predecessor, Maitoa, had also once accorded me. "Welcome!" He peered at my cap. "I've never seen a crown like that."

Should I say it? "The Lady Pua made it for me, my lord."

He roared in laughter. "Mine too! Mother does good work." He faced Va'aru. "Can we eat now?"

In this company, I was well down the hierarchy but not too far. I wondered if my priestly feather cap gave me some extra points. Or did it have just the opposite effect, mark me as being of a certain caste, rather than some unknown quantity as an 'hero from the sea?' At any rate, I allowed the attendants to place me where they would. Ve'eta, of course, took the first place and Va'aru, as our host, the second. Hei'iro, being a king, was next. After them, I could not say, but there were a couple more before Hareata, and a half dozen or so between me and him.

Beck, as the adopted son of a noble and another who had come from the sea, sat directly to my right. Our Beka, despite his fair coloring, was looking more and more the Mora warrior he had become, with a full compliment of tattoos now displayed on his massive frame.

The rest of our party were commoners and did not eat with the High King. I must assume Rika and the others would find their ways in this place.

"I wonder when Temani'itu will show up," whispered Beka. The old sailor had taken an interest in the younger one and the two had spent time together, exchanging tales and smoking. Were the High King's uncle here, I would assume the fourth place would have been his. He was probably still sitting on Hareata's porch and drinking Hareata's beer and wishing he were with his fleet. Eventually, duty would bring him to this place.

"Hareata might know," I answered. "They do not confide all their plans to me."

Beka furrowed his brow at this. "They should," he said, and turned his attention to a baked plantain. The boy put more faith in me than I was inclined to myself.

As the diners dispersed, drifting away in small groups, Hareata came to Beka and me, saying, "Ve'eta will not call for you today." He glanced toward where the young High King sat, listening to a circle of men around him. "But Hei'iro would like to speak with you." As we rose, he added, "Marareta only, my friend Beka. But I think the High King will wish to see you both tomorrow."

I followed him outside, where King Hei'iro stood on the high porch, gazing out over Aedina. I was quite surprised that he greeted me as had the High King, as an equal. Hei'iro was known for his strict formality and adherence to the ways of old.

So he must regard me rather highly. Whether that was a good thing or bad, who might know?

The king was one of those men who can not stay still. He constantly fidgeted, shifting his weight back and forth, turning his eyes here and there. "I thank you, Taona, for bringing my son back from across the mountains." Was there a slight smile on his round face? "I also thank you for taking him there. He has become the hero I hoped he would."

"He was my right hand, my lord."

"And he helped you win the daughter of Arierona. I think it for the better he did not wed her himself." He cocked his head at me. "Is this a good woman he has chosen as his wife?"

How best could I put this? "She has become one in this land, sir. Amirea, I believe, has found the strength that was always in her."

"Good. Aranu needs a strong hand." Hei'iro chuckled. "I know this. And now Rahaita is yours, eh?"

"The daughter of Arierona is not yet wed to Marareta," spoke Hareata. "At least not by the rites of our people."

"Then they should wed, and soon," the king stated. "You need to quit hoping to match her with that young blockhead."

"I know well how you feel about our High King, Lord Hei'iro," said Hareata.

"Then remember also that I voted against him. But High King he is and I accept this. I am not like Revaru, to murmur of rebellion." His expression told me he had a low opinion of his fellow king, former ally or not.

I could also read relief in Hareata on hearing these words. I knew he had mistrusted this man's loyalty.

"Ve'eta listens to that fool of a High Priest," continued Hei'iro. "A mouther of empty words. But I would speak of the words you sent from A'auwa, Hareata, the words of Pana'a." He looked intently at me. "And of this man's part in them. Are you the hero from the sea?" he asked me.

"I do not know, my lord. I believe the prophecy but could not say whether it speaks of me or another."

Hareata nodded in approval. "Taona Marareta is most definitely an hero and most definitely from the sea. But there are others who came with him and have also proven themselves."

"One accompanied you, did he not?" Hei'iro did not wait for an answer. "And another remains at the house of Arierona. I have heard of him and know he is too an hero."

I would not mention yet others, who now resided in the north. They had not drawn much attention to themselves and would probably prefer I did not either. The king went on. "We must take seriously what is told us by the gods."

He believed the prophecies of Pana'a to be some sort of divine revelation, then. I had no intention of trying to change his mind, even though I knew their actual origins. We both believed in their truth.

"That we must," agreed Hareata. "But now, my lord, let us sit and hear all the tale of Marareta's adventure, and that of your son, beyond the mountains."

And they did, there on the porch of Va'aru, there by Aedina.

19. Ve'eta

"There was far more to your journey than I had realized," said Hareata. He had not before heard the complete story, though I knew parts of it had reached him. "I might fear the numerous people of that valley, were not the high mountains between us."

"Your own people are a more present danger," I replied.

"That they are. We are a warlike folk, Marareta, and too often we have warred upon ourselves."

"There is no need. You have not begun to fill up this land and there is much more in this world," I said. "There is plenty for all."

It was raining on Aedina this morning. We sat on Va'aru's porch and watched the showers pass across the lake's surface. "I am sure Ve'eta will ask for you sometime today," said the Mora nobleman. "Both of you."

"Soon, I hope," said Beka. "I'm tired of watching water drip from the eaves. I can do that at home."

"It rains more here," I told him. I thought it did, anyway. The weather in this land was a bit tricky, on a northwestward facing coast in the tropics, and with those high mountains. James Nathan had worked out that we must be ten degrees or so north of the equator.

"You have not yet seen one of the great storms that comes out of the sea," Hareata remarked.

"I think one of those brought us here," I told him. "But that was born in our own world."

"The legends of my people tell the same story."

"I wouldn't be at all surprised if the Kohari had a similar legend."

"They do not like to speak of the sea," said Hareata. "They believe demons dwell there and the evil are consigned to its depths."

"Kohari come here sometimes, don't they sir?" asked Beka.

"Since the war, none have been allowed above the Great Falls. I believe there are traders even now on the beach below them." He looked toward a stir near the entrance to this house. "Ho, this is unexpected."

It was Ve'eta himself, with a small retinue, walking toward us. He held up a hand to prevent his attendants from following him further and dismissed Hareata with a movement of his head.

"My lord," said Hareata, and retreated to a discreet distance.

"Sit down," said the High King, as we rose to greet him. He plopped down in the space Hareata had vacated.

He stared at Beka for several seconds. He'd never seen him before, had he? "We would be cousins, now," said Ve'eta. A wry smile came to his face. "Definitely an improvement over my other cousins."

Third cousins, right? Did Beka knew of their relationship? "My mother has told me of this," he said. "She has tried to drum all our family's genealogy into my head."

"I would rather create the next generation than worry about the last," stated Ve'eta. He looked at me. "I had hoped I might do that with Rahaita."

"Um, my lord —"

He held up his palm. "No, no, that is alright, Taona. There are many other women and certainly some of them like me better than the daughter of Arierona." He leaned in closer. "But it is politics. My advisers say it would be a good match and help create stronger alliances. And Rahaita is very beautiful —

"But be that as it may. If she will not have me, then there is no shame to being bested by an hero. An hero and a priest. That is a strange mixing, Taona!"

I wondered how much of this he had memorized and rehearsed before coming to see me. There was something of Lady Pua's cunning here, but he was also more simple and open than his mother. I couldn't help liking the boy, even if we were to be rivals.

"My lord, I did not choose to be either. Sometimes things are thrust upon us."

He nodded. "They are, aren't they? I do not mind being High King but I wish I could have waited a few years." Suddenly, he laughed. "I wish you had become my mother's third husband. I would like you as a father!"

And with that, he abruptly rose and left.

Beka leaned in and whispered, "He's an odd one, isn't he? I like him, though."

Hareata stood watching his High King until he had reentered the house of Va'aru. Then he came and sat again with us.

"I will not ask what words Ve'eta spoke to you," he said. "It is enough that you parted with smiles." He looked out over misted Aedina. "I would suspect those canoes bring Temani'itu and his retinue to us."

I turned to peer in the direction of his gaze. Two large dugouts. Yes, those had been drawn onto the shore near the house of Hareata.

"Hero from the sea or not, you will be left out of many of the meetings of the next few days."

"Arierona named me his envoy," I reminded him.

"This is true, and you could demand to be present. That would only make enemies for you, Marareta. But," he continued, "I shall make certain all know of your status here." Hareata frowned slightly. "That undercuts me, of course, if it is known you have his support. They will assume he also approves of your marriage to his daughter. Which perhaps he does?"

"Perhaps," I admitted. "In honesty, Lord Hareata, he would not say one way or the other."

"Arierona is far more wily a politician than most realize. I think, too, this latest prophecy has set him to viewing things differently." He rose. "I shall go greet the High King's uncle. You may not see me again today."

20. Over the Falls

"Lord Temani'itu would like me to go to sea with him."

"What do you think of that?" I asked Beka.

"I do not think I would want to be away from Miruhata so long. But it would be good to at least look upon the sea again."

"I would enjoy handling a sail myself." I had not since I had been on the Lake of the Sky, beyond the mountains. "But I might like it just as well on the waters of A'auwa."

"We are no longer sailors, are we, Marareta?" No, we were not. We had found new loves.

For sailing had indeed been a love, for me, in the world from which I had come. It was one of my few enjoyments, an escape from my pointless and passionless life amid the society of New York.

"Is the admiral leaving soon?" I asked him.

"Tomorrow, even if he has to leave things unresolved here. He says he has had enough of this place."

I nodded. This agreed with what Hareata had told me. I had, indeed, not been invited into most meetings, official or otherwise, but was deemed important enough for people — and I say people, for some of those here were women — to seek me out and ask my views on this or that. As the potential son-in-law of King Arierona, it was best not to ignore me.

But as the possible hero from the sea, there was an uncertainty about me. Some feared me, I think, some thought perhaps they could use me in some way. Ve'eta again sat down with me and had me repeat the entire story of my jaunt beyond the mountains.

"That should be an epic!" he told me.

"I have a friend who is working on that," came my reply, and I wondered how Ulani was progressing.

"I wish I could have such an adventure," Ve'eta then sighed. "I shall never be in an epic."

"One never knows. We could have an infestation of dragons or another Kohari incursion. Or Koharis riding on dragons," I could not resist adding.

"Ah, then we would have to have some of those griffins of which you told me," he replied, falling into the spirit of the idea.

I got the feeling that little had been resolved at this gathering, which had been haphazard and unplanned from the start. Most of the kings had stayed away, busy with their own affairs, and there was little agreement as to whether a few priest-led commoners were any sort of threat. Ve'eta's most trusted circle of advisers seemed to think not.

And, ultimately, advising Ve'eta had been the point of coming together. As for Ve'eta himself, I think he just wanted a vacation from the boredom of the house of the High King. This accomplished, he now prepared to return home — return home without any promise of a wife, which had been his other hope.

"There is no reason we should not accompany the Lord Temani'itu to the coast," I told my friend. "I must find Rika and tell him."

"Rika's a good man," Beka allowed.

"He is." Courageous, as had been all the Mora who had crossed the mountains with me, but also the most astute of that band.

"Lord Hareata has not told me of his plans," I went on. "With Temani'itu leaving and Hei'iro speaking of doing the same, he will be without his two strongest allies here." It was apparent these had formed a triumvirate of sorts, in support of the High King but in opposition to his current advisers. Even among the Mora, politics tended to make for strange bed-fellows.

"If Ve'eta goes, there's not much for him to do, is there?"

Maybe not, but a politician must always be minding his connections and alliances. "He's not likely to head back to Arierona, so I would think we were on our own."

"Then we can visit at the coast a few days and then head home. That sounds good to me."

"Me, too," I agreed.

Within the hour, Hareata informed me that he was accompanying the High King to his house. What he hoped to accomplish there, he did not tell me. I was quite willing to remain ignorant.

The next morning we were ready to board Temani'itu's canoes and depart. These, however, were already quite crowded with men and baggage, and no others were readily available. "We *could* squeeze in, maybe," Rika said.

I looked across Aedina. "Let's just swim over and take the trail to the falls, " I suggested.

"Yes," agreed Rika. "but our packs would get wet."

"Throw them on the canoes, then. We won't need them right away."

Beka, however, did not like this idea at all. "I don't swim very well, Marareta. Not well enough to get across here."

Rika and I, being strong swimmers, had not even considered this. "Then we must fit into the canoes," I said. "It is a rather strong current, anyway." I would not wish to take a trip over the Great Falls — though there were lower falls before one reached those.

We ended up perched on the baggage for the rather short trip, angling across the lake. At docks near the lower end of Aedina, all had to be unloaded and carried the rest of the way, along a trail paralleling the river as it went over lesser falls on its journey to the final, high drop to the sea. Temani'itu made this trip in a palanquin; I did not envy those who bore the massive Mora.

Then we stood atop the cliffs, looking out to the wide ocean, the Great Falls roaring to our left, and a broad bay lined with wide sand beaches below us. Many vessels were drawn up onto those beaches, canoes large and small, and even the boxy boats of the Kohari.

21. Music

"It is long since I was able to clamber down a rope," said Temani'itu. So saying, he reclined into a large basket, to be lowered to the sand below. The rest of us descended upon the dangling lines.

There were many huts on the sand, but a strict rule prevented them being built too close to the cliffs. That might aid a potential invader. "Every now and then, bad storms and high water wipes out most of what we place here. Even the canoes may be lost, " Temani'itu told us.

I surveyed the wide, shallow bay. Yes, a typhoon would wreak havoc here; there would be no safe place and even those huge canoes we had sailed to raid the Kohari, more than a year past, could be destroyed.

"The best thing is to fill the canoes with stones and pray to any gods that might be listening. Here is where we dwell. Do not name it the house of Temani'itu. It is the house of all those who sail upon the sea."

It was in fact an exceptionally large, open thatched hut, low and simple. Many smaller but quite similar huts stood close. "There are no women, my lord?" asked Rika.

"They may come and go as they wish," replied the admiral. "Few remain the night, and those are usually sailors themselves."

"Women sailors?" Rika was skeptical, though Beka and I knew better.

"Fisherwomen, mostly, busy about the work of their trade. You would do well not to annoy them, boy." We entered the long hut that was not the house of Temani'itu. Here and there a mat hung, an attempt to create the illusion of a room, but mostly it stood open. I could see men reclining in hammocks, or sitting in groups. The only fires burnt outside, on the open sand.

"I must call my officers to me now and have their reports," said Temani'itu. "Wander where you will. The Kohari traders are across the lagoon, if you should wish to see their wares."

Wander we did. There was quite an expanse on which to do so, but not much of note to look upon. A dugout canoe is a dugout canoe, even a very large one. All these were of a single hull, with outriggers; I remembered from somewhere that some South Sea islanders built double canoes. I might mention the idea to Temani'itu or someone else in charge of such things.

Across the lagoon — the lagoon being the space below the Great Falls, dividing this beach in half — I could see the squarish Kohari boats. These were built of planks, unlike the single log dugouts of the Mora. I had never seen one up close, but knowledgeable Mora had told me they were stitched together with palm fibers.

We stood looking across the lagoon. "Is it safe to swim over?" I wondered.

Beka stared, as if trying to see beneath the surface. "There could be crocs."

Saltwater Crocodiles could certainly find their way here from the mangrove swamps further north. I felt nervous just standing this close to the water.

"Sharks, too," offered Rika.

HERO FROM THE SEA

At that point, a Mora woman, short, sturdy, and smoking a cigar, strolled past and took pity on our ignorance. "You may cross under the falls," she told us. She smelled very much of fish beneath the reek of the tobacco.

Sure enough, there was a solid, if damp, pathway behind the falling water. Many Mora and their canoes were on the far side too, along with the camp of the Kohari traders. A stillness fell on that camp when we drew near it.

Then voices speaking low, some in Kohari dialects, some in the trade pidgin.

"The men from the sea," came one, and, "The ones who burnt down the temple!" spoke another.

"And good riddance to it," mumbled one of the other voices.

We were recognized. And, it seemed, not universally hated. Those who traded upon the sea were not overly concerned with the affairs of priests and warriors, goddesses and temples. Travel, they say, widens one.

As the Mora, these men and women were sheltering within several open huts. I could see more huts and more Mora further beyond, spread along the beach, and both canoes and Kohari boats drawn up onto the sand. One of the men, a paunchy fellow with a graying beard, came forward to greet us.

"I welcome you to our camp, lords of the Mora," said he. His slightly mocking expression belied his respectful words. "I suspect that curiosity brings you to us." In other words, we were not paying customers.

"True enough, sir," I replied. "We have nothing to trade."

"Then we shall offer you only hospitality. Though I do have some excellent flints here." I had wondered just what the Kohari brought here, and what they took home. We followed him to the nearest hut, where he turned and said, "You are those who came from the sea, are you not? The ones the Mora believe to be some promised heroes."

I shrugged. "We are supposedly mentioned in one of their prophecies," I answered. "We know little of such things." Don't give me that look, Rika. "We were but castaways, brought here by the storms of the sea."

The Kohari laughed. "Very well, my lord. Come and share a meal with us. I am named Poyo." He indicated a middle aged woman seated by a small fire. "My wife, Nawita. Some of my sons are about here too."

I gave him my name as Mika, as the Diwarna had called me when I first came to this world, and introduced my companions. Beka's family, I recalled, kept many Kohari slaves, captives of war, so he was comfortable around them. Those slaves were treated well and always freed after a time; many chose to remain.

And many married Mora women. The father of Heho was just such a man.

Rika was a bit shyer of these alien folk, but soon sat eating with us and making eyes at a girl who brought us bowls of the palm wine of which the Kohari were fond. "One of my sons' wives," commented Poyo, though she seemed barely old enough. That women married young in their male-dominated society seemed likely.

Other Kohari gathered about us, drawn by curiosity, no doubt. "I met one of your people on the far side of the mountains, " I told them, thinking a story might ease our acceptance here. "He named himself Bato."

"A common name," one said.

I nodded. "Bato was quite an old man, who escaped the priests while still a youth."

"Good for him," spoke another, and spat. I took this as a sign they would be sympathetic and gave all of Bato's tale. Soon, many tales were being told, both by the Kohari and by me, as the afternoon slipped into dusk.

Torches were lit. "Let us have music," said one of the men. "Get out your sef, Poyo."

The sef proved to be zither-like and oval in shape, with three strings and decorative designs carved upon it. I had noted the Mora had no stringed instruments, only flutes and drums, and had in an idle moment mused on the idea of building a harp.

Obtaining a sef, had I known of them, would have been more practical. The songs these men gave us, to the rhythmic plucking of the sef's strings, were more melodic than any I had heard in this world. They sang, of course, in dialects of the Kohari language, which shared much of its vocabulary with the pidgin. Therefor I was able to follow the meaning after a fashion but probably missed any poetic element altogether.

Something about a cockatoo; I caught that. And a girl — "girl of the palm trees," I believe. Then a shriek. It took me a few seconds to realize it was supposed to be call of the cockatoo, repeated at the end of each verse. I am still not sure whether the song was intended to be romantic or humorous. Perhaps both.

Soon, a pair of women rose and began to move through the steps of an intricate dance. Rika looked as though he might like to join in, but Beka put a hand on his arm. "Kohari men do not dance," he whispered. Mora men did, and quite readily.

Then my friend Beka did something that quite surprised me, raising a rich baritone on one of the sentimental songs of our far and forever lost home. Poyo quickly caught onto the tune and managed an accompaniment in something resembling the right key.

They might not have understood the words but from that moment the Kohari men saw us as brothers. It was late when we stumbled back to the house of all those who sail upon the sea.

22. Ahurataca

Temani'itu sat listening to the words of a messenger. Then he called us to him. "I sail and you will wish to sail with me," he told us. "To Ahurataca we sail."

The point marking the end of the cliffs along the sea, and the northern boundary of the Mora. "What is there, my lord?" I asked.

"The son of Hei'iro," was his reply. "Or he soon will be." No further explanation followed.

"Then we sail with you, Lord Temani'itu," I agreed, and my comrades nodded in assent. The largest of the canoes were kept by the lagoon below the Great Falls. Launching these was no easy matter, even when they rested already partly in the water, requiring many men and many ropes. We pulled with the rest, getting Temani'itu's 'flagship' off the beach. The flow of river water through the wide lagoon helped in this task.

Fortunately, there were none of the crocodiles we had feared in the shallow waters, as we waded, up to our waists, at the work. I believe one might have been able to wade right across that lagoon. Some of the Kohari came down to the water's edge on the far side and watched us at our labors. I could not catch their words but I would assume there were rude remarks.

Then we were under sail, the two woven mats catching the wind and carrying us north. No one had needed to even pick up a paddle.

The Mora were fine sailors, that is certain. There were a score of us, all told, on that canoe, and it could readily have held half again that many men. If going to war, it probably would, but we had no need of warriors right now.

We sped northward. If Aranu awaited us, I could understand bringing him back in this manner. It would take many days less than were he to walk south through the realm of Anana. And, too, none would see him save us.

It takes days, not hours, to sail from the Great Falls, the entrance to the Mora homeland, to Ahurataca, even with the most favorable winds. Then the high white cliffs rose to our right. "We're back to Dover, Marareta," said Beka.

"Dover?" queried Temani'itu.

"It is a place of similar cliffs in our homeland," I informed him. "It reminded us of it when we first glimpsed these walls."

"Dover," he repeated. "I like the sound of the word but it is nonsense in the Mora tongue."

"It sounds like the Kohari word for wisdom," said one of his men.

"That it does," Temani'itu agreed, "and the Kohari are wise not to approach those cliffs."

I knew the cove that lay before us. It was where I had first set foot on the Mora realm, before joining Temani'itu's great fleet that sailed to attack the Kohari. A small outrigger paddled out to us, a single man in it.

"Hito!" I called.

He looked up at me, apparently surprised by my presence. "Taona. We had barely arrived when we saw this great vessel. Did you come for us?"

"We did. You and Aranu?"

"And Heho," he answered, as he climbed aboard. "He had to show us his secret pass through the hills." He lowered his voice. "It is too dangerous to use the other way."

"All are friends here," I told him. "You may speak as you will. Lord Temani'itu," I said, turning to the massive nobleman who had stood patiently beside me, "this is Hito, one who accompanied me across the mountains."

"My lord," said Hito.

"If Aranu is ready, go fetch him," ordered the admiral. "There is nothing else to keep us here."

"You stay," I told the warrior. "I'll paddle in and get my friend." I noted he wore his short bronze sword, the only one we had brought back from the Valley of Visions. The other Mora had deemed them too heavy to haul across the mountains. Into the little canoe I hopped and paddled toward the beach.

I could see men coming down ropes from the clifftop as I approached. Heho and Aranu helped me pull the canoe onto the sand, beside several others. Fishermen ventured from this cove into the ocean, sharing it with those who watched and guarded the coasts.

"Marareta!" cried Aranu, and embraced me mightily. Heho chuckled.

"You were unexpected, Taona," said he. "It is good to see you but now I must return to my duty."

"You do not come with us?"

"No, I have messages to bear to the house of the High King." Without further word, he turned back toward the cliffs.

"Heho barely escaped the rebels on his way north," Aranu told me, as we pushed the canoe back into the surf and clambered aboard. "There is much happening and I thought my place should be in my homeland." Another Mora, perhaps the vessel's owner, climbed in with us.

And so we had come for him. Making this voyage to pick up one man — Hito didn't really count, but was only along for the ride — seemed extravagant but I realized it was part of Temani'itu and Hareata's effort to retain the good will of Aranu's father.

"If the messenger had not gotten through or none awaited us here, we would have gone south on foot," he continued. We paddled toward Temani'itu's great canoe. "I had expected a much smaller vessel, if any."

"I spoke with your father," I told him, "at the house of Va'aru. He is not nearly so fearsome as I had been led to believe." Aranu laughed for some time at that. Then we boarded the larger canoe and sent the smaller home.

"Lord Temani'itu, I greet you," he said.

"And I you, son of Hei'iro," responded the old sailor. A smile split Temani'itu's craggy face. "I hear you are to marry."

"No, my lord. I am already married. It seemed the thing to do before going off and leaving Amirea."

"You did not wait for me to officiate?" I chided.

"Oorto did a perfectly good job. He was good enough for you, after all."

Already, the great outrigger was turning for its trip home. "Then, as with Taona Marareta, you will need to have a proper Mora wedding later on," Temani'itu told him. "Do it close enough to the coast and I shall attend."

"I would be honored, my lord," responded Aranu. "We sail to the Falls?"

"We do."

And then what, I wondered, and how soon might I return to A'auwa?

23. The Quartz Knife

"Your father lingers at the house of Va'aru," Aranu was told. "He was preparing to leave when he heard you were on your way."

The young Mora noble nodded at the messenger's words. "Then it is to the house of Va'aru we shall go," he announced. "Do you journey there, Lord Temani'itu?"

"Not a chance of it. It would take a very large storm to get me back atop the cliffs."

There might be such a storm coming, I thought, but not the sort of which the uncle of the High King spoke. There was no real reason for him to return to Aedina now, though.

We feasted that night with Temani'itu and his sailors, and in his long low open house there was little notice given of rank. Men sat where they would, for they were all brothers on the sea. "The laws and taboos they follow up there," one Mora sailor told me, gesturing toward the east, "do not extend beyond the cliffs." I am not certain all agreed with that attitude, but enough did.

In the morning we set out, we five, for Va'aru's house, climbing the ropes let down for us and taking to the well-worn pathway. As we walked, Aranu filled us in on events in the north.

"Heho showed up wounded," he told us. "Not badly, but scuffed up a bit when a group of men pelted him with rocks. They were angry and outsiders make a good target."

"Angry about what?" asked Beka.

"Everything, it seems. Isn't there a bridge somewhere around here? I remember crossing it when I was a boy." I had heard that such a bridge existed, some distance above the High Falls, but none of us knew exactly where to turn to it, so we trekked on. "It has become dangerous to follow the trade road through the lands of Mahutunoa," continued Aranu. "Pua fears this may turn into a full rebellion."

I had to ask, "Are they safe at the village?"

"I would think so. But without trade there is no reason for the village to exist."

When we reached Aedina, canoes were waiting and we were taken across immediately. We were expected. They would have been disappointed had we located the bridge and crossed there.

The Mora tend to be affectionate, effusive even. There is much embracing. Not so with Aranu and Hei'iro. It must be admitted, however, that Aranu's father awaited him at the entry to the house of Va'aru, his fellow king and host at his side. Demonstrative Hei'iro might not be but I have no doubt of his love for his son.

It was near the noon hour, then. "We must have a feast of welcome for your son tonight," asserted Va'aru. "But let us lunch now. He and these," he swept a hand toward me and my companions, "will sit in the places of honor." Nothing all that new for Beka and myself but quite a promotion for Hito and Rika to even sit with kings.

I am not certain Hei'iro quite approved of it but it was, after all, Va'aru's domain. We all sat to eat one of the king's simple lunches, which would be deemed a feast in most places. Servants came and went, bearing baskets of fruit, bowls of starchy pastes, platters of pork and fowl. The beer, too, flowed into our cups.

Beside Aranu I sat, his father to his left. On my own right was Beka. Something seemed to catch his attention.

He jumped to his feet, even as a man, seemingly one of the servers, rushed upon Hei'iro where he sat.

"Traitor!" the man screamed and jabbed with a shining knife. A second later, Beka had him on the floor.

There was blood, a pool forming about the supine Hei'iro. A great gash could be seen on his left side and seeing that gash relieved me greatly, for it lay across several ribs. It had not penetrated between them.

No cloth was readily at hand so I doffed my own loincloth and pressed it against the wound. It should be stitched up eventually, but to stanch it now was enough. Hei'iro opened his eyes and burst into laughter to see me, naked, dabbing at his side.

"Aiee, by all the gods, that hurts. Do not make me laugh again, Taona!"

By that time, those better suited to such tasks had come and I left the king to them. But I would never be able to wear that loincloth again. I turned my gaze to Beka and the would-be assassin. A pair of warriors had hold of the man now, an older individual than the knife-wielding boys of my previous incidents.

His knife lay on the floor. I noted this blade was of a yellow quartz, not rose. Maybe they ran out of the other kind.

"Here, Taona," came a voice at my elbow. Va'aru himself handed me a clean loincloth, which I fastened about me. It was somewhat large. "I shall have everything he knows before he is executed." The affable king's voice held an unaccustomed edge.

"He was nearly as inept as the last two of his sort I encountered," I said.

Va'aru agreed. "Priests, most likely. Certainly not warriors." He paused. "I would have gone for the throat."

As would I. "I think he intended to reach the heart. Maybe as a symbol."

"There is no stronger symbol than death," said the king.

24. Parting

"I would not be completely surprised to learn that Revaru had a hand in this," said Hei'iro. "Not directly but in encouraging those fanatics to believe I had betrayed them." The king lay on a mat on his right side, while a physician finished stitching up his left. He gave no sign of the pain he must be feeling.

"Who saved me?" he asked. "Someone tackled that assassin, I know."

"It was Beka, Father," answered Aranu.

"Ah, then I must thank him." He looked at me with something between a smile and a grimace. "As I must thank the Taona for the donation of his loin cloth. Not quite so heroic a gesture, but welcome none the less. Ow." He barely mouthed this last, an acknowledgment of his pain.

"You're done? Good. Someone bring me beer. Much beer. And a large bowl so I don't have to get up to piss."

I decided that was as good a time as any to exit Hei'iro's sleeping chamber. Somewhere, Va'aru was undoubtedly questioning his prisoner. I doubted he would go to any extremes on that until the intended victim was able to ask his own questions. I would expect Hareata to hurry here, as well.

I did not particularly want to stay until he arrived. As soon as proved practical, I would head up the Teoma toward A'auwa and my wife.

It was not yet dusk. I wandered from the house of Va'aru and down to the Lake Aedina. It was both different from and alike

A'auwa. Smaller, with a swifter current — little more than a widening of the Teoma, in truth. There was no wild land left about it, no forest, and many docks with canoes and rafts tied to them. But when the light of the setting sun fell across it, I could almost imagine myself on A'auwa, Rahaita at my side.

After a while, Beka joined me. "You intend to leave, don't you, Marareta?"

"You know me, my friend. Are you ready to go home?"

He said nothing for a time. "I think I shall stay with Aranu for a few days. He says his father asked that I would."

"Don't dawdle too long. Miruhata will blame me if you do." We both turned and walked back toward the house of Va'aru. "So it will be just Rika and I traveling north."

"I should not be too far behind you," he promised. "Maybe Aranu will come too."

"If we could get Amirea to the house of Arierona, he would be sure to come."

"You could have a double wedding, as Poneiva and I did!"

That was not an unattractive idea but I did not plan to wait any longer than necessary to marry Rahaita according to Mora customs. I doubted we could get Amirea and Aranu there together anytime soon.

In the morning, I informed Va'aru of my intentions. He nodded but made no comment. Of his prisoner, he did speak. "He would tell us much if he knew anything. He is only a rural priest who came under the spell of this Tahu."

"He called Hei'iro a traitor as he struck."

"Yes. Those who take the traditional ways to an extreme feel he has betrayed them by not rising against Ve'eta." He shrugged. "But to Hei'iro, supporting the chosen High King is the height of tradition."

I was not sure I wanted to know, but I asked, "What will become of your prisoner, my lord?"

Va'aru raised an eyebrow at me. "This question is one that has arisen before, isn't it? What was it Maitoa did?"

"He said there were two crimes, one against me and one against his hospitality, and asked me to choose between burying my attacker alive or having his head bashed in."

"You chose the latter. Strictly speaking, since that was the punishment for his attack on you, it was the only one you had the right to choose. You would not have known that and I doubt Maitoa cared." He seemed to think for a moment. "We have the same choice here. The crime against my house and the crime against Hei'iro. I will say, a clubbing is much less trouble than digging a large hole."

"Except that Maitoa then buried the man alive after he was slain." We both laughed at that, Va'aru saying it was very like the late High King. "His successor will never have such subtlety," he lamented. I did not see that as necessarily a bad thing.

Later I made my goodbyes to Aranu and to his father; early the next morning Rika and I were paddling north out of Lake Aedina and up the broad Teoma. We traveled in one of the many canoes that were always available on the rivers and streams of the Mora nation for use by couriers or for anyone on more-or-less official business. Few abused this privilege but it was very broadly interpreted.

A red symbol, painted near the prow, marked this as one of those canoes. Every canoe used here had many markings on it, just as the Mora people bore their many tattoos, designating ownership and petitioning one deity or another for favor. I had begun to learn to decipher these marks but might never understand all their nuances. They were as complicated as the Mora language.

"We are making good time," said Rika. "We should pass Lord Hareata's house before dark. Will we stop there, Taona?"

"I would rather not," I replied from my place at the stern. "It would delay us."

"The Lady Panoha might enjoy delaying you."

"All the more reason to hurry by," said I, to Rika's laughter.

But it was not to be. As we approached the village near the house of Hareata, I spied a woman with a girl at her side on the river bank. She waved at us.

Panoha. "We are recognized," I sighed. "It would insult her and Hareata not to stop now."

We directed our canoe toward the shore.

25. Panoha

"A rumor has come that someone tried to kill Hei'iro," spoke Panoha, as we walked up the path toward her home.

"It is true. I was there." I wondered if the sister of Hareata had known we were coming and waited by the river. "The king was wounded but recovers. I suspect," I added, "your brother is rushing to the house of Va'aru even now."

"This is most certain, Taona. Hareata must be in the middle of whatever is going on." She turned and smiled knowingly. "I think you are trying to do just the opposite."

I had known Panoha was a more intelligent woman than some credited her as being. She had displayed a sort of quiet wit at our previous encounters. Perhaps being in the shadow of such men as her brother and the late High King had led her to keep her thoughts to herself.

Her rather large little girl, quite evidently the daughter of Maitoa, walked behind us, with Rika. Lady Pua might have looked much like her at that age, which I guessed to be about ten.

Panoha herself was not a small woman. Beside her brother, she did not seem very tall, but at my side I could see her to be of above average height, within a couple inches of my own. She was plump but far from obese; a substantial person, as was Hareata, and a handsome enough one, in her way.

Mehetu, her sister-in-law, came forth from the house of Hareata to give us welcome. She had probably been in on the scheme to get me here.

HERO FROM THE SEA

Without the master of the house there, our evening meal was informal. The Lady Mehetu even invited Rika to sit with us, perhaps hoping for conversation. Rika, however, as Panoha, was not a particularly talkative person, more inclined to listen and make the occasional remark. It was for Mehetu and I to fill the silence, and we did not always manage that.

I did give the tale of all that had happened since last I saw them, the occurrences in Va'aru's house by Aedina, our voyage north to bring Aranu home. "So Beka saved Hei'iro?" asked Mehetu.

"Possibly. The assassin's thrust might have gone askew anyway."

"The knife of golden quartz is interesting," said Panoha. "Those are used by the priests of Wanga, aren't they?" she asked Mehetu. Wanga, I thought, was some sort of sea god.

"Yes. So it is not just the followers of Te'eta who are involved."

Panoha addressed me now. "The priests of the Red Sky once practiced the sacrifice of humans with their rose quartz blades. That has long been prohibited."

"Since the days of the first High King," Mehetu said.

"I have heard such tales," spoke Rika. "I did not know whether to believe them — our priests do not seem at all bloodthirsty."

"It is different in some corners of our land," stated Mehetu. "I do not know if the followers of the Great Shark practiced such sacrifices."

"I have heard Wanga demanded men sometimes. Women, too. They would cut them so they bled and then cast them from the cliffs," Panoha informed us, her voice subdued.

Rika shook his head. "It is good we do not live in those days!"

114

"It would seem there are some who wish to bring them back," I told him.

Although the house of Hareata was not overly large, its gardens were extensive. Torches were lit and Panoha and I strolled there after our meal, among the citrus trees, hung with large yellow-gold oblong fruit, and the flowering bushes and palms.

"Do you not grow bored at this house?" I asked her.

"I like the peace after dwelling with the High King. There was always so much going on about Maitoa! And Mehetu likes having me here. She grows very lonely with no child here and Hareata often gone.

"Hareata and Mehetu have no offspring?"

"There is a son but he is now older and at the house of King Anana." She sighed. "I loved Maitoa, Taona, and he gave me Tita. I do not fault him that he was not able to give me more children."

"Who can explain why such things happen?" I remarked, trying to be both philosophical and noncommittal.

"It was because he grew far too fat, and old before his time, Marareta. That was not difficult for me to understand." That would teach me not to try to sound wise. Tita came out to us as we walked, to bid her mother goodnight.

The girl cocked her head at me. "Are you going to marry my mother?" she asked. As direct as her Aunt Pua, too.

"I have pledged to marry another," I told her. "There will be no talk of such things now." I was being politic, of course, and had no intention of pursuing relationships with other women after my marriage.

That seemed to satisfy the child, who hugged her mother and left us — but not before giving me a long, appraising look.

"You will have no other woman," asked Panoha, as we walked further, "even for the companionship of a few hours?"

The torches were far behind us now, and I looked upon her by the light of stars, blazing by their thousands. "No, my lady, there is only Rahaita for me, until all things are resolved."

"Then I suppose I should not find my way to your room tonight."

It was best that had been averted now, rather than later. But I chose not to sleep in my close, windowless room that night, anyway, instead stretching out on the porch by the gardens. There, I slept well.

As we prepared to leave in the morning, having breakfasted with Rika there on the porch, Mehetu came hurrying out to us.

"Revaru has been slain!"

26. Revaru

"A messenger just came with the news, sent south by Va'aru."

"He is still here?"

"Yes, but must leave soon to carry it further. All the way to Arierona."

I recognized the man, had seen him bearing messages before. He was taking a quick meal before continuing his journey. "Tell me of this," I asked him.

"The king was stabbed in his own bedchamber, as his wife lay beside him," he reported. "A priest, it is thought. The assassin was slain by the guards when they heard the screams and ran to him.

"That is all I have, Taona," said the messenger. "But Heho asked me to tell you he is now at Aedina, awaiting the Lord Hareata's arrival. He thought it likely we might meet on Teoma."

"I thank you and will detain you no more." I went outside and looked upon the gardens for a minute or two. Rika came to stand by me.

"Do we turn about, Taona?" he asked.

"There would be no reason," I replied, "and perhaps all the more reason to hurry home."

We made our farewells and were upon the river within the hour. It seemed we traveled faster than the news, for no one gossiped of Revaru or Hei'iro at those places we stopped. Certainly, though, official messengers were swiftly conveying knowledge of these events to the kings and great nobles.

There was talk among the people of Tahu, the priest who seemed to head the disgruntled traditionalists. Some supported him; most saw him as a madman. In the more distant reaches of the Mora homeland, it might well be the opposite. There was a dissatisfaction among many of these people, a fear of change and of outsiders, and a dislike for an isolated High King who seemed to have no thought of them.

We passed the Teiri and I thought, for a moment, of those far to the north in the trade village. I thought also of the young High King whose house lay not so far to the north. He would be tested by what was coming, by what was already happening. Could I — could any of those who had come to this world with me — help him in this? Would one of us truly be the hero of prophecy?

I rather wished someone else would wash up on the shore and take the job.

Mostly, I thought of the one who awaited me by A'auwa. Would Arierona approve our marriage on my return?

One has too much time to think while paddling. And there was some distance yet to the realm of Arierona. To our left, lay lands of the High King; to the right, those of Avatu. Rich lands these were, prosperous lands, and not yet overcrowded.

Long and uneventful days later, we reached Arierona's kingdom. It would not be much further to a fall that would force us to either portage or take to the road for the rest of our journey. For most travelers, it was not worth returning to the river for a few more miles of paddling; those who used Teoma between that fall and high Pana'a at the mouth of Lake A'auwa were generally local.

As we neared that spot, Rika, again in the bow, pointed toward the right bank. A group of men stood there, warriors by appearance. I recognized their leader.

"Lord Ponu!" I called, holding up a hand in greeting, as we approached them.

"Taona Marareta," he responded. A pair of his men helped pull the canoe ashore. "I give you my greeting and that of Arierona. A messenger who came before you with news of Revaru's death told also of your coming." Ponu, nephew of Arierona and likely heir, was, as the king, a man of ordinary size and stature, with dark heavy eyebrows that met at the middle.

"Beka is not with you?" he asked.

"He remained at the house of Va'aru with Aranu and Hei'iro," I told him. "Beka will find his way back soon, I am sure." I looked for his brother Poneiva among the men but he was not there.

"Ah, yes, Hei'iro owes a debt to Beka, I hear."

"It is so. We should continue toward A'auwa." Were we to have an escort?

Ponu only nodded. "We shall tend to your canoe and see you there in a few days time. My cousin awaits you." He looked at my companion. "Your wife, too, Rika. She does not know why you ran off again so soon after being gone the better part of a year."

Rika stood himself up straight and answered, "I would follow the Taona Marareta anywhere, my lord."

"Not into my bedchamber, I hope," I told him. "Let's head on home."

27. Wedding Plans

"If I did not approve of this, I know Rahaita would be ready to accompany you into exile. She would find a way, even were I to forbid it.

"I most certainly could not force her marry another. Not that I would wish to do so."

And so Arierona was giving his consent to our marriage. I had been at his house only a day before he had drawn me aside to make this declaration.

He continued. "We shall announce your wedding for a month from now." He thought on that. "We shall have to check with the astrologers for the ideal day. Anyway, that will give any who wish to attend ample time to travel — and you, ample time to prepare."

I knew something of those preparations, the ceremonies and purges and such. I would probably learn more. More than I wanted.

"Now," he said, "give me all the tale of your travels. Everything, even the petty politics in the house of Va'aru."

It took more than an hour, or two, to give that tale, for the king had many questions. We went to his veranda and ate as I continued it and then walked in his garden. "So," he said at last, "it might seem the attacks on Hei'iro and Revaru were two parts of one plot. It is odd they attacked those kings who were friendly to their cause."

"Not friendly enough, sir. Neither would denounce the High King."

"Hmm, yes, for some, only complete commitment is enough." I had known such fanatics in my own world.

"Isn't there another king," I asked, "who voted against Ve'eta?"

"Hara'a. We hear nothing from him." He smiled and clapped me on the shoulder. "I have kept you long enough from my daughter. Go tell her of my decision. Not," he admitted, "that she did not know I would give in eventually."

I found Rahaita with my son. Our son, soon, perhaps. "Your father says we must make wedding plans," I told her.

"Marrying you once was enough for me," she replied, coming and wrapping her arms about me. "But if Father insists on a second wedding, so be it." Rahaita pulled back and looked at me. "Whom should we choose to officiate?"

"Will any priest do?"

"Almost any. You can't perform the ceremony yourself, naturally."

"It would save some trouble. I wonder if Samua would be interested. He's considered a priest now, isn't he?"

"I am not sure. Every holy man is not a priest." She brightened at a sudden thought. "We should find a priest of Teva!"

If I remembered rightly, Samuel had actually been ordained by some sect or another, back in the world from which we had come. He could in fact perform a Christian ceremony for us, if I wished it.

Now, I had been brought up Christian myself, of course, but there seemed no point in bringing that to this world with me.

Samuel could preach of Jehovah to his fellows on the island; I would just try to do what was right.

Finding a priest of Teva sounded right to me. Maybe he could even give some pointers on how to do the job.

As in the world in which I was born, invitations must be sent before a wedding. Strictly speaking, that was Arierona's prerogative but he was quite willing to let us do it. "Just be sure to invite all the kings," he warned us, "even though none are likely to come. We wouldn't want to offend any of them."

"Aren't we short a king now?" I asked him. "Who replaces Revaru?"

"The nobles there should elect an eligible nephew or cousin. He will have to be approved by the High King, but that almost always is just a formality."

I put most of the nobles I knew on the list — a figurative list, as the Mora had no writing — and Rahaita added a far greater number that she knew. "What of the commoners?" I wondered. "We know some of those too." Heho came to mind, and Rika.

"They must be in the entourage of some noble guest or another. Just tell them to come and then assign them to somebody. I suppose it is not possible," she said, "to get invitations all the way to the trade village."

"I *would* like to invite Lady Pua," I admitted.

"She came to our first wedding," Rahaita reminded me.

"Lord Hareata, of course, and his wife. I hear he is coming to see your father anyway."

"He can even bring his sister, if he wishes," she announced. Maybe she liked the idea of Panoha witnessing our marriage.

"And I hope Aranu can make it."

"Yes. It's too bad we can't manage that double wedding."

And so we continued. I am sure we invited far, far too many.

Soon after, Heho appeared at the house of Arierona. "Hareata will come along in a few days," said he. "I have been sent ahead with messages."

"Be sure to stay for our wedding feast," I told him, as I escorted him to the king.

"If I can, Taona. Things are falling apart. There is turmoil in the kingdom of Revaru and they can not decide on a new king. The road across the hills is nearly impassible. The warriors of Mahutunoa make some effort to guard it but they have other concerns, ones the king deems of more importance." He went on into Arierona's chamber to make his reports.

I went elsewhere and thought on what he had told me. "I fear for our friends on the far side of the hills," said Rahaita, when I filled her in.

"I do not know if there is any place safer," was my reply. "That is why they were sent there. And, if trouble should come across the hills from the lands of the Mora, they can disappear into the jungles and wild lands further north. Oorto can guide them to safety."

Rahaita nodded. I hoped that I was right.

28. Teva

We found our priest of Teva, an old fellow who tended a shrine across A'auwa. He seemed happy to know others were choosing to follow his deity. "The flashy gods get all the young men, the ones that promise glory and honor. How can rain and simple love compete with that?"

"I would choose those two anytime," I told him.

"You must have the proper tattoos," he said. "Teva knows you are a priest without them but no one else will." He looked at the two hearts on my arm.

"Those are counted emblems of Teva in my home. The leaves that, um, the rain causes to grow."

"Look more like hearts to me," he answered. At any rate, I went under the needle of the tattooist again and had the proper design emblazoned across my right shoulder. And I had her add a vine connecting my two hearts so they might look more like leaves.

Then, a king came. That king was Ruapata, who ruled to the east of Arierona, beyond the Teoma. There was much open country there and it was there Arierona's men had battled those of Nesmith when he had kidnapped Rahaita, a year previously. It was through a corner of his land, too, that we traveled on our way from the High King's house to A'auwa.

The king also brought his wife. "I shall be honest, my brother," he told Arierona, "I fear the troubles on my borders. I would ask that Va'ai might dwell in the house of Arierona until these matters are resolved." Some of those borders were shared with King Hara'a, who, it was rumored, now harbored the rebel priest Tahu.

Perhaps that was the only reason Ruapata had come to our wedding — two weeks early, it must be noted — but I would not complain about having such a guest.

The next week, came another king and that king was Hei'iro, borne in a litter as his side was still stiff. With him came his son, and Hito and Beka, and our old friend Hareata. No women, however, accompanied them. I was not sure whether or not I was disappointed.

So the wedding of Rahaita and myself was turning into a council of war. At times, I sat with these men who debated and made plans, but my thoughts were on my wife, not on politics.

"Revaru tried to play both sides and it got him killed," Hareata told them the first evening they all gathered. "Tahu or his followers saw him as a betrayer."

"There are rumors Mahutunoa is losing in his battles against the rebels," said Ruapata, "and that warriors of Hara'a fight along side those rebels."

"And what is our High King doing?" Hei'iro asked. "Listening to advisers who tell him all is well?"

Arierona would not have this. "I think Ve'eta will do what is needed. This is not like an incursion of the Kohari, where one can see his enemies before him."

Then Ruapata had to have his say again. "Last year, I spoke at our council, saying the office of High King should perhaps pass to another house. That was a ploy of politics, as you know, but I feel there may be merit to the idea."

"And now, as then, I say that my house has no claim on nor desire for the High King's dais," countered Arierona.

"And I hope need for such a change will not arise. But we must be prepared if it should."

With this, all were agreed.

There were only a few days now until the wedding and I must undergo various rituals. I must also forgo Rahaita for a short time — which felt like far too long a time. She, too, had ceremonies to attend to. Would she swim in the Pool of the Moon, as her cousins had more than a year before?

And who might serve as her guide? I could not on this visit, obviously. A male family member would typically accompany the bride-to-be, a symbolic protector. Maybe Ponu? Well, that was for her to choose.

At loose ends, I went to sit by A'auwa once again. I had done that often, before so many things had changed. It was nearing evening and a cool breeze rose from the lake. I could see two figures seated near the shore, gazing out toward the Sacred Island.

"Welcome, Marareta," spoke Pana'a, as I neared them.

"You know this boy, my lady?" asked the old priest of Teva.

"Very well, my friend, very well."

"Ah. Perhaps it is you who turned him to the service of Teva."

She laughed. "Perhaps so. But I only turned him. It took another to cause him to step toward it."

I sat down beside them, Pana'a between me and the priest.

"Then it is good he is marrying her," said the old man. "I have married thrice and it was good every time. Well, maybe not so much the second one — but it was still better than having no wife."

Pana'a looked at me and there was sadness in that gaze. "It is never good to have no one." Then she turned her face to the sky and laughed. "Perhaps you can make it rain on me, priests of Teva!"

29. We Three

"Three kings at your wedding! That is something to boast about," said E'eva.

"One is father," replied Rahaita. "He doesn't count."

"Even so. He was the only king at ours."

"And that was only because you are our best friend," added Miruhata.

Both Rahaita and I knew better than this. The girls were part of the king's extended family and he would have been there for them, however his daughter felt about it.

My wife — who was also my future wife — turned and told me, "I have prevailed upon Samua to be my guide to the Pool of the Moon. Only his devotion to you, Marareta would make him leave his island.

"Are you coming with me?" she asked her cousins.

"Oh, yes," E'eva said. "And Teme wants to come too. Our husbands will be subjecting the Taona to his purification rites."

I could have made many remarks but I only chose to embrace my wife. "Thank you for thinking of Samua," I whispered. "I shall see you when I am allowed." With that, I left.

Those rites, I knew, were not all that demanding. A bit of fasting, some time in a sweat lodge. I had sense enough to drink a great deal of water first. And, most likely, I would drink a great deal of beer after. But not too much — there would be a wedding to attend the next day!

HERO FROM THE SEA

Rahaita and her friends would be off to the Pool of the Moon this afternoon, so she might swim by the light of the rising moon. And I would be sweating around the same time. A few hours open before then — when would Samua be coming over from his monastic isle? I could see if he had arrived.

Then, I believed, I was supposed to engage in some sort of ceremony involving chanting. Not allowed to eat during any of this either. That was no great hardship; all this was not unlike making weight for a fight, something I had done more than once in the old days.

I strolled along the path by A'auwa, looking north toward the island of men. Yes, there was a canoe making the tricky landing at the near end. The current was strong there, just above the fall of Pana'a. Then it embarked again, a passenger aboard. I waited for them.

Why, that was Beka at the paddle. Going to pull in just a little further up, are you? I was there in time to help pull the canoe up onto the bank. "Samua!" I embraced the old fellow. So thin!

"Mr. Malvern, sir," he said. "Reporting for duty!" He gave a reasonably crisp salute. "What's the agenda today, sir?" he asked. All of this was in English.

We both stared at him until he began to giggle. "Ha, had you there, Taona," said Samua, reverting to Mora. "My mind is still in one piece. And I have peace of mind, too, mind you!"

"How are you, Samua? Are you up to a long walk with my wife this evening?"

130

"If not she'll have to carry me. I wouldn't mind being carried by a bunch of pretty girls. Wouldn't mind at all." He looked out toward the isle from which he had just come. "No girls there, and that's good, most of the time. But not always! No liquor either and that is always good."

"And, I suspect, nothing to talk about so you're getting as much of that in as you can."

"Ha, true enough, sir. We mostly talk to God out there. One god, just like Christians. I wouldn't have gone otherwise."

"I'll take you to the house, Samua," said Beka. "Our Taona is not allowed to look at his bride again until tomorrow."

"Ah, I checked the rules on that," I told him. "It's allowed to look at her from a distance. But I can't get close or be in the same house or talk to her or — well, do anything else I might want."

"Poneiva will come and take you to your rites as soon as we get our friend squared away. And mind you, Samua, keep away from the beer. I know what happened the last time they let you off the island!" They walked off together toward the house of Arierona.

I sat and waited by A'auwa, drinking water. That too was kosher during my fast. I had made sure to check — not that I cared about the rules but I would not jeopardize my wedding coming off on schedule. It was not only Poneiva and Beka who came to collect me later, but Aranu as well.

"We three will make sure things are done right," said Poneiva. "I think you might be inclined to cheat if we let you, Taona."

"Since he considers himself married already, he thinks it doesn't matter," Aranu told his friends.

"It probably wouldn't matter to him even if he weren't married," Beka added to this critique. "He's just that sort."

He was pretty much right about that. I was never averse to stepping on my opponent's foot if the referee was distracted. No low blows, however; one must draw the line somewhere.

So I chanted and I sweated and I starved, just a bit. It would be worth it. But it would have been better if those three hadn't been outside the sweat lodge, drinking beer and making rude comments. That's the problem with being a decade older than your closest friends.

And when it was done, I lay down on the cool grass beside A'auwa with those three friends and slept, dreaming of Rahaita.

30. At Last

I remembered how tired Beka and Poneiva had seemed on the morning of their wedding. I felt invigorated, as though I had been in training and was now ready to go fifteen rounds for the title. Middle-weight. Hmm, yeah, I probably still was in that class.

No beer for me. I went straight to A'auwa and dove into the waters, getting a good drink while I was at it. Why, I felt good enough to swim out to the Sacred Isle and suffer the consequences for stepping foot on it. Death by crushing had Pana'a told me? Perhaps not.

I needed a clean loincloth. I thanked Teva there was no need for more formal wear here. Did I *own* another loincloth? I had still been wearing the oversize one Va'aru had lent me. Shouldn't I have thought of this earlier?

And should I wear my little feather crown? Didn't Rahaita have some sort of crown as a princess? I remembered — yes, and pretty tall. It would make mine look quite pitiful.

Maybe I did need some beer. I walked, dripping lake water, toward the house of Arierona. There was Samua. "Well, you're quite a sight, Taona. I think I need to be your attendant once again, if just for the one day. Come along." I followed him in.

"I'm starving, Samua! Let's get some food first." He looked annoyed but led the way toward the porch. Preparations were already being made for the feast there. The busy servants took pity on me and loaded me up with an armful of fruit and a bowl of beer. I followed Samua back into the house.

HERO FROM THE SEA

I was too busy slurping and swallowing to pay attention to where we were going. Nowhere near the quarters Rahaita and I shared, of course. "Here we go," said Samua, leading me into a small room. "All laid out and ready for you." I stared at the pure white loincloth, the cloak of feathers, the tall crown. "Costume for the groom," he announced. "There's one about like it for your bride. You wouldn't want to put it on for a few hours yet."

"Well, you have eased a great many anxieties I had, Samua. A few hours — the ceremony is at dusk, isn't it?"

"No sir, at noon. Didn't you know?" I had assumed it would be the same as Beka and Poneiva's wedding. "That priest Hoka insisted on it."

"Maybe his third wife wants him home before dark." I sat down on the floor and ate my breakfast.

The Mora nation might be falling apart around me but I did not care today. I might worry about it next week sometime. Yes, I was already married to Rahaita but this made it all final, removed any doubts, and those friends who could not be at my first wedding ceremony were gathered for this one.

A couple hours later — I am pretty sure I napped — I slipped into those fine garments and made my way to the gardens of Arierona. There, Hareata, of all people, wearing his own feathered cape and crown, took charge of me. So he was to be the equivalent of my best man? I couldn't have chosen better, if anyone had bothered to mention it to me. The nobleman led me to a large flowered bower where stood the priest of Teva. "Isn't this much nicer than when it's getting dark out?" the old fellow whispered to me. I had

134

to admit it was. "I won't fall asleep during the ceremony, either," he chuckled.

As I had been led from one side, to stand in that bower, Rahaita had from the other. Yes, dressed as I she was, but I think it looked much nicer on her. Her step-mother was the one who accompanied her, Arierona's second wife, with many garlands of red blooms about her neck. I tried to follow the simple and brief ceremony but I shall admit I was far too distracted. I would have to get the priest of Teva to teach it to me sometime. Then we were led to the feast.

Rahaita and I had the high place at that feast, Arierona at my right, then Ruapata and Hei'iro beyond him. I was told later those two tossed dice to see who sat the higher. Three places down on our left, just beyond the wife of Ruapata, sat Pana'a. I remembered that she would perform some blessing or rite as we retired to our bed chamber, ostensibly to consummate our marriage. That might be a little awkward for all of us.

No doubt that feast, and the singing and dancing and games continued long after we slipped away. No doubt people ate and drank too much, made new friends, fell in love. No doubt they were happy, but we were happier.

Pana'a stood at the entry to our room, a crown of hibiscus on her black hair. "I hardly think you need this blessing," she said, "but I shall give it to you anyway."

HERO FROM THE SEA

May love fill your lives,
may life come of your love,
we ask of Mother Moon,
this night that comes but once.

Did she wink, oh so slightly, on that last line? Then she spread white blossoms, gardenia, I suspect, on the threshold. "Emblematic of the moon, of course," explained Pana'a. "You two would recognize that. And they smell nice." She let her eyes linger on us for a few seconds. "That is all. Now get in there."

She turned on her heel and disappeared down the hallway.

Part III. All the Land

31. Rewards

"All those who followed you across the mountains are gathered here now," spoke Arierona. "All those who brought my daughter home."

With Aranu and Hito here, that was so. "I must reward them," continued the king. He gave me a knowing look. "You have received the only reward you wanted, I believe, but you should have some higher station as Rahaita's husband. A wandering priest who owns nothing is not what I had in mind for her."

I knew well that my wife had no qualms about having married a poor priest. We had already spoken of settling at the shrine of Teva, on the far side of A'auwa.

"And," said Arierona, "if you should take a second wife, you must have some way to support her, as well." Like others here, he thought that I would marry Panoha eventually. Her brother Hareata seemed quite sure of it.

"I think, my lord, that Rahaita is the only wife I shall ever want."

"Oh? It's all the same to me, my son." He had taken to calling me son since the wedding, though I was closer to his age than that of his daughter. "But the bond to Hareata's family could be a good thing for both of us." Hareata's family would include the king Va'aru.

Indeed, Hareata would have been eligible for that kingship. The fact that his cousin was chosen over him possibly stemmed from Lord Hareata's outspoken views on many subjects. It should be noted that a son of Panoha, should she bear one, would also be a potential king. The Mora woman was no older than I, so it was certainly possible.

No wonder Arierona favored the match, even if I were already wed to his daughter.

"I shall award the warriors lands," he said. "Would I could make them nobles." It had been assumed I was noble from the time I arrived in this land and I had been willing to go with it. Though, as a supposed priest, I was also in a special category, neither noble nor commoner. The only way to ennoble commoners was for them to marry women (status being inherited through the female line) of a higher caste, or for a noble family to adopt them. That latter was how Beka became a noble of the Mora, and was not uncommon.

"They will have high rank among my men, too, if they wish it." Hito might like that. The rest, I felt, would as soon put the ways of the warrior behind them.

"As for Aranu, I would welcome his presence among my warriors, too. But he has a wife now, far away." He raised a questioning eyebrow. "Would he choose to live across the hills with her?"

"I do not think either he or Amirea would wish to remain there."

"Yes, Amirea. She is as ambitious as any noblewoman of the Mora." Which was saying something. "I would like having them here. I welcomed her family to my house as nobles, so she and her children will be accepted as such." He nodded in satisfaction, having settled that in his mind. "Your status has been clarified, too, Marareta, both as husband to Rahaita and truly a priest."

My new tattoo had apparently made my vocation official. "You could remain in my house and serve me. I welcome your advice on all things; this you know.

"First, I would know of this." He picked up the bronze club I had brought him from beyond the mountains. "Of what is it made? And could we find this substance here?"

"It is created by the mixing of two kinds of, um, stone. Whether either is to be found near here, I do not know, but I have seen one of them used by the Kohari." Copper ornaments were not common among them but neither were they rare. Where one would find tin, I had absolutely no idea. "My friends beyond the hills might have more knowledge of such things."

"Neatanu?" That being the name by which J.L. Nathan had come to be called.

"Perhaps. Or his retainer known as Dutsa." Then I thought of another, one who was much closer. "Oh, I was forgetting Bafa, my lord. He might well know more of such things than any of us."

"Bafa is clever, that is certain. Brave, too." And as likely as any to be the one named in the prophecies. "I shall ask him of this." He lifted his eyes from the weapon to peer at me. "And I ask of you if you now intend to adopt Maratoa as the son of Rahaita."

"That is our intention. Pana'a approves."

"How could she not? It is certainly best for the child."

Yes, but best for Pana'a? The old priest of Teva had told me he had seen her sobbing by the shores of A'auwa on our wedding night. She had returned to her island now, and her duties as priestess.

"The time has come to turn our attention outward," spoke Arierona. "Ruapata prepares to return to his house and Hei'iro speaks of traveling to speak with the High King. Perhaps I, too, should go forth."

"To Ve'eta?" I asked.

"Yes, to Ve'eta. The High King should hear a new voice."

32. A Loss of Balance

Arierona had not hinted that I might accompany him north and for that I was thankful. What could I do there, anyway?

The latest messages said Mahutunoa had suffered a defeat and been driven from his kingdom. The king had fled across the Teiri to take refuge with Anana. The carefully balanced power structure of the Mora kings had fallen over.

These people had no sense of history. I knew that nations came and went, that all things changed. For them, the past was largely the place of legend, nebulous, inhabited by heroes and gods.

Although they were spread across a wide land, the Mora were not really that numerous. Only a handful had come here, centuries earlier — nine great canoes, said the legends. Some claimed the houses of the nine kings arose from those.

How many centuries it had been, none could say, but it must have been many for the population to have grown to its current size from that modest group. That they had been fruitful and multiplied was obvious, and that they had warred among themselves in those early days was remembered. That they had mixed with earlier inhabitants, including the Kohari, I also suspected, though most would have vehemently denied such a thing.

And I mustn't forget that probably every one of them carried the heredity of Hurasu, the ageless sorcerer who dwelt in the Valley of Visions. That man was unquestionably an ancestor of Rahaita and Pana'a, and it was from him they had inherited their powers.

HERO FROM THE SEA

Of Pana'a I had seen nothing since the day of my wedding. Rahaita, however, I rarely let out of my sight. "I thought to visit the shrine of Teva," I told her. "Would you like to go?"

"I think not, Marareta. E'eva and Miruhata are spending the morning with me."

"They could come if they wished." I doubt I sounded enthusiastic about that idea.

"I would not inflict them on old Hoka. Say hello to him for me." Old Hoka just might enjoy being visited by young women, I thought but did not say.

To A'auwa I went. Should I paddle across or walk around? If I walked, this would be an all day affair. I had first seen the shrine when Rahaita and I and the warriors who accompanied us from the north had made our return to this land. It lay toward the south end of the lake, near where Teoma flowed into A'auwa.

Once since had been I there, when I sought a priest of Teva for our wedding. Then I had approached by water. I started walking south; if it grew too late, Hoka would have to put me up for the night. The Mora are big on hospitality.

It was more wooded near the head of A'auwa and I enjoyed walking in the shade and I enjoyed having somewhere to go. I need not get there quickly though. Perhaps I would indeed settle by that shrine with Rahaita, be the priest there when the old man went to Teva. I could think of far worse futures for us.

Across the suspension bridge I went, the river rushing below. Not too wide was Teoma here, but deep as it gushed through a high-banked gorge. It must already be near noon. Then back to the north, along A'auwa's shore. There was the shrine, set deep into the trees, easy to miss.

Teva. The statue, carved of dark wood, said little of the deity except that he obviously enjoyed making love. I went past the little garden in which it stood, to old Hoka's hut. Two women dozed on the porch; it was siesta time and I could have napped myself.

The priest himself sat quietly smoking before his home. "My wives," he said, waving his pipe toward the pair. I had thought it unlikely any were still alive, much less two of them. One no more than middle-aged, as well. "What can I do for you, Lord Marareta?"

"You can never call me Lord again," I told him, settling by his side. "I am only your acolyte when I come here." And no one called me Lord, anyway.

"That you will never truly be, my boy. You may serve Teva but your place is over there." He nodded in the general direction of Arierona's house.

"Among the powerful? I weary quickly of them, Master."

"And when you do, come visit. Pana'a and the other priestesses sometimes paddle over here. It is more private than the house of Arierona and they may speak more freely with me than with those who dwell there."

"I was not aware of that. You have known Pana'a long?"

"I knew the woman who was Pana'a before her. And I loved her. Ah, that was an age ago, Taona!" The title Taona I was willing to accept, though I would still have preferred none. "Your Pana'a —" He chuckled. "Yes, yours, I know this. Your Pana'a was here only two days ago to seek my wisdom. Or maybe it was my wine that interested her. Would you like some?"

"Certainly, Master Hoka." I was rather hungry too but said nothing of it. He brought a wooden bowl, filled near to the brim. "When my wives awaken, we can have a meal. This, I make from whatever fruit happens to be ripe." It was not bad and probably no stronger than the beer I was accustomed to at Mora meals.

Hoka's voice came suddenly serious. "Pana'a speaks of your son as being an heir to prophetic power."

Maratoa would have gifts? Had she sensed this? Seen it? I knew not what to say.

"Your wife has such gifts, doesn't she? Her aunt says she may be the most powerful she has ever seen." The old fellow shook his head. "She says also she has more control over them than she had ever imagined possible. Take care they do not take her from you and make her a priestess.

"But the boy — there has never been a place for such among our people. Priests are not seers. Or they do not admit it if they are." Was he hinting he had known such men? "That island out there, Pana'a's island, is a place of power. It might not be wise for your Maratoa to grow up too close to it."

"If he has gifts, he can be trained to use them," I said.

"Maybe." He sounded skeptical but I had learned much of such things. Oorto could certainly teach the boy, if his mother could not. I knew also that talents were typically latent until one approached maturity. Sometimes a good bit later.

"Ah, my wives yawn and rise. We can eat." He looked to the sky. "It is growing late. Would you stay the night?"

"Not that late, Master. I would not mind walking home in the dark."

"If Rahaita awaited me," said Hoka, "I would hurry home at any time. But then, I would never leave in the first place."

The priest made sense. This shrine was not the place for me, even though it offered all I had said I wanted. I could not hide away, forgetting the needs of my wife and of my son.

I would have to find a balance.

33. Positions

"Civil war has broken out in the kingdom of Revaru. What was once the kingdom of Revaru," Hareata corrected himself. "The nobles have split over a successor, different cliques naming different choices, and now fight each other, as rebels push into their land from the north and east."

"The High King should pick one of the choices and support him," stated Hei'iro. "One who is strong."

"One who had the cunning of Revaru might be better," replied Hareata.

"We see where that got him," answered the king.

I decided to say something. "Isn't that getting close to the home of Ve'eta?" They were headed for that home, after all.

"It is," spoke Arierona. "I think I should take more warriors than I had planned." This might be turning from a diplomatic mission into a military one. "You should send for some of your own, Hei'iro."

That king's expression was sour but he nodded an agreement. "Maybe Ruapata can spare some men."

"That I doubt," said Hareata. "He may be driven from his home, even as Mahutunoa was."

Arierona scowled. "I hate to take men away from the defenses here. I have to trust you, Ponu, to keep safe my house. And you too, Marareta." He turned to Hareata. "Heho is on his way?"

"An hour on the road by now, my lord. Ve'eta will know we come."

"I hope he realizes now that there is trouble in his realm," Hei'iro said. "I shall send word to my land and have a troop meet us at the house of the High King." Overland, to the west, it was not so far from the home of Arierona to that of Hei'iro. He had come here the long way around, up the Teoma.

"Very well," spoke Arierona. "We leave, then, in the morning."

"Your friend Beka will go with them," Ponu informed me as the group dispersed. "Hei'iro asked for him."

"Does Aranu travel with his father?" I asked.

The man shook his head. "No, but Bafa goes with some of his archers."

I didn't see enough of Bafa these days. We were brothers-in-law now, officially. Hmm, I was related to this man by marriage, too, and to Poneiva and Beka, who were wed to cousins of Rahaita. I would have to sort out all these new relatives in my head.

That in itself was a warning to steer clear of Panoha, had I any thoughts in that direction. An alliance there would bring all sorts of complex kinship into the mix. I would be related to pretty much everyone!

Aranu had been placed in a position of authority among the troops, true to Arierona's word. He was still a quite young man, younger than Poneiva, too young for high command. This latter preferred to be a noble retainer, a sometime warrior, rather than commit full-time to the service of his king. Trade and the managing of his family's estate were more important to Poneiva.

One day, that estate would pass to one cousin or another and Poneiva might find need of a place among the warriors. Or the re-

sourceful Mora might be off to the Gurang again, to trade for crocodile hides, or he might even become the sort of diplomat that
Hareata was. Beka would be inclined to follow him, wherever he
went.

I watched the kings march away the next morning, a full eighty
of Arierona's men accompanying them. Hito came and stood at
my side until they disappeared into the north. "What have you
been up to, my friend?" I asked him.

"I am once more a warrior of Arierona. Aranu named me his
second," he told me, "and none objected."

That was a position of some authority, akin to being a master
sergeant in the world from which I had come. As a commoner, he
would not be expected to rise any higher. "Now," he continued, "I
must find myself a wife. I had no chance with Amirea against that
boy."

"Any prospects?" I inquired, as we turned and walked toward
the training grounds. Those lay behind the house of Arierona, and
to the north — well away from his gardens on the other side.

"Too many, maybe! I have met more than one I liked during my
recent travels." He lowered his voice just a bit. "Some of them noble."

"You are considered a hero now. I think no one would greatly
object to such a match." A moment of further consideration led
me to add, "Our Heho certainly did well for himself."

"That is so, Taona. But I shall probably see none of them again
soon." He sighed. "If ever."

In a change of subject, he asked, "Is it true Rika has become your personal retainer?"

"He has. Why he wished it, I do not know. He could have had a position like yours for the asking."

"He is tired of being a warrior. All those who passed over the mountains were." He laughed, a bit ruefully. "I know nothing else to do with myself."

"Well, Hito, you were the only one unmarried."

He shrugged. "True enough, Taona. I had less to return for than the others and might have remained if any else had." Hito lifted his eyes toward the mountains, distant in the east. "I have sometimes thought of going back." He laughed. "But I think it would be easier to find a wife on this side of the mountains!"

He joined the men exercising with their weapons. I watched him a while, thrusting and chopping with his bronze sword, the only one west of those mountains. Then I went and looked for my own wife.

34. Wives

"I shall send no warriors of the king's house," stated Ponu. That he was resolute in this, no one could doubt.

It was understandable; Arierona had charged him with the safety of his home and family. "I will ask the nobles, however," he said, "to raise men."

"I would be willing to do this," said Poneiva. "It will take time."

"And I," spoke another noble there, an older man whose name I did not remember. Or perhaps did not know. Others in the group assembled before the house of Arierona expressed agreement. Whether they would follow through was anyone's guess.

A messenger had come, exhausted, from Ruapata, begging for aid. The king was harried and beaten by the rebels who had invaded his land from both the north and the west. "There were soldiers of both Mahutunoa and Hara'a fighting along side the rebels," reported the man.

"I name you, then, Poneiva, to lead those who would go," spoke Ponu.

"Send messages, all of you," Poneiva told them. "Call what men you can to assemble at the head of A'auwa and we shall march from there. In two days time. No longer!"

Many couriers left the house of Arierona that day, some sent by nobles staying there, some by Ponu himself. I returned to my wife and my quarters, thinking my part done.

Va'ai, wife of Ruapata, was with Rahaita. I think Va'ai must not have been much older than my own wife, so it was not surprising she would go to her. A rather slight woman she was, and I do not think I had heard her say more than four or five words since she arrived.

This was to change. She turned to me as soon as I entered and demanded, "Do you go with those who will help my husband?" I looked over her shoulder to Rahaita. She gave me a quite firm nod.

"I shall," I replied. "I guess I should break the news to Rika."

Rika's status had become something between that of a steward and a bodyguard. I might not have accepted his service if I did not now have a family to protect. It would be useful to have him around, I felt, and his wife too. As a part of the king's household, I did not have to worry about providing for them out of my nonexistent means.

"Thank you, Taona," she said, with considerable sincerity. "Lady Rahaita." Out of the room she hurried.

"I am not sure this is altogether a good idea," I told Rahaita.

"Your wisdom may be needed, husband. And do not look at me like that. You are wise whether you will admit it or not!"

Well, if they only asked for my advice, it might be alright. I was not eager to fight in yet another war. "It is only your love for me that keeps you from seeing the fool I truly am," I answered. "And I guess I could not disappoint Va'ai."

"She loves her husband greatly. Ruapata took her as a second wife, but his first died soon after so now she is the only."

"And he cares, too. I could see that when he brought her here for safekeeping."

"They are not unlike us in age," mused Rahaita. She smiled rather impishly. "You know, I would not mind you taking a second wife. Maybe I could get more things done if you were not always underfoot."

I knew, though Rahaita spoke lightly, she actually meant it.

"Would you then take a second husband, my dear? Hito is in search of a wife."

"Hito? Mmm, no, but I can think of some names for him."

"Make them nobles. The man wants to move up in the world." I had sensed that bit of subtext in our conversation.

Rahaita became suddenly serious. "There may be many noble widows soon," came her subdued voice. "War is upon us."

Many of those who assembled to go to the assistance of Ruapata were noble. Young males of such birth were commonly fighting men, men who had no more wealth to their names than most commoners. These tended, often, to serve in the houses of lesser nobles, rather than with the disciplined troops of the kings.

They would come to the service of those kings when called, however, as they did now. Better than three hundred fighters had come together on short notice, and others would certainly be following. Poneiva left a lieutenant where Teoma met A'auwa to gather any latecomers over the next couple days and then march after us.

Why Poneiva? He knew this eastern country and Ponu was aware of it. The young man was also recognized as a competent and respected leader.

One can not forget, though, that he was moreover the son of a major noble house. No Mora would ever forget it, anyway. It was a good thing that boy could live up his heritage.

From the head of Lake A'auwa it was not very far at all to land where Ruapata was king. The fighting, however, we assumed would be on the other side of his realm. "Best to march to the house of Ruapata," spoke Poneiva, "and from there to where we are needed."

Rika marched beside me, carrying one of the stout Mora thrusting spears. At his waist dangled a relatively dainty stone ax, its head an exceedingly sharp blade of flint. It was a good weapon for a man of his ordinary stature.

Ponevia, too, carried an ax but its head was a massive piece of polished green stone. I had seen the same stone used for the making of clubs. My own wooden club, the one given me by Arierona when I first sailed with him against the Kohari, was ready at my side. With any luck, I would not be called upon to use it.

But use it I would, if needed. I had fought battles on the other side of the mountains, and battles crossing them, as well. Too many battles; I was weary of fighting still. I had hoped for peace and for rest on my return to the Mora homeland.

One of the scouts who had run ahead came hurrying back to us now. "Men. There." He pointed northwestward. "Not soldiers of Ruapata, I think."

"I will go straight to them," said Poneiva. "Marareta, take ten tens and circle to the east." So I was to be his second in command, not just give good advice.

HERO FROM THE SEA

It turned out to be neither rebels nor soldiers, but refugees.

35. Ruapata

"They burnt all the huts," the old man told us, "and killed our priest."

"Where did these murderers go?"

"Eastward," was the reply, and the ancient pointed in more or less that direction. "We sought to go to A'auwa to find the protection of Arierona. We knew not where else we might turn, my lord, nor if Ruapata yet lives."

Poneiva looked at the tired and frightened faces of the group, women, children, mostly. "That is wisdom, Grandfather. Lead them there." To me, he said, "The rebels move toward the house of Ruapata."

"If there is to be a battle, we should be part of it," I stated. I did not like what I had heard of these rebels.

"Unlike Mahutunoa, the king is not one to flee. But he might fall back to the protection of the mountains." He turned again to the leader of the refugees. "How long?"

"Only yesterday, my lord."

"Then we must hurry," decided Poneiva. "Come!" The Mora warrior began jogging toward the east and we followed. No more than three hours later — that was always a guess in a world without timepieces — we heard shouting from ahead.

"Battle cries," said a warrior near me. "They are exchanging insults and challenges," spoke another. Soon we spied them from a low rise.

HERO FROM THE SEA

There was no discipline to speak of here, only two angry mobs facing each other across the rolling open fields. That would be Ruapata and his men over there, decidedly outnumbered.

"Take your men around again," Poneiva told me. "We shall show ourselves and attack on this side."

I and my hundred hurried to the north, trusting that distraction and a small hill would prevent us being spied. The rest of our force hurled itself on the rear of the rebel army. I could not see, but from the sound of things Ruapta's men charged their enemy as well.

Now to add to their confusion! In we drove on the unsuspecting left flank. Not to boast, although that is the prerogative of a Mora warrior, but I think it made the difference in this battle.

Let it be said these were fierce and skilled fighting men on both sides, and no battle between such might be easily won. Spears found bodies, clubs and axes rose and fell. But mixed with the warriors we faced were less experienced rebels, commoners who had little practice with their weapons. Those were not slow to break and run, creating disarray in the ranks. Three loud blasts of a conch trumpet echoed over the battlefield.

"That is a call to throw down their weapons and receive clemency," Rika told me. "Ruapata is merciful."

And didn't want to lose any more men for no reason. It was obvious we had won the day. I watched opposing warriors drop to their knees in surrender. Only here and there a knot of fanatics wished to fight on. Those were shown no mercy.

Ruapata and Poneiva were already conferring by the time I reached them. The king glanced at me and then turned his attention back to a captive. A noble, I could tell, from his tattoos. I had gotten better at reading those.

"It was the priests who ordered it," he was telling them.

"The ones who follow Tahu?" asked Poneiva.

He spat. "Tahu preaches somewhere in the west. It is Hara'a who commands."

Ruapata nodded. "So it is certain, now. I had suspected this."

"I have never seen this king of the east," Poneiva said.

"He rarely leaves his own lands," responded Ruapata. "I met him only once, when all the kings gathered last year. You were there, Taona," he said to me.

"I was, my lord. He was the third to vote against Ve'eta, was he not?" I had departed by that time. I remembered him as being rather young, and rather handsome, but also aloof. He had something of a dreamer about him.

"He was. Yet he said not one word in the debates." The king shook his head. "His uncle was not so."

"Then he wishes to make himself High King," mused Poneiva.

"Perhaps the only king," was Ruapata's answer to that. "That and to bring the old ways back."

We had gathered the prisoners together by then, and set them to clearing the bodies from the battlefield, the dead to be burned, the wounded to be tended, if possible, dispatched if not. Not surprisingly, many warriors displayed a willingness to take service with us. They were fighting men who asked only a lord that they might follow.

Of these, a number were men of Mahutunoa who had gone to Hara'a after their king's defeat. These Ruapata was willing to take to himself. The warriors of Hara'a's house showed less enthusiasm for changing sides.

And the rebels — those few who survived or who had not escaped — both Poneiva and Ruapata distrusted. Any who had not surrendered when the others laid down their arms could legitimately be executed. "I'll take them home as slaves," said Poneiva. "That will get them out of the way." Ruapata was agreeable to this, and did not even ask for any compensation. He owed the house of Arierona for many things already.

That left a handful of rebels who had accepted clemency. "Neither of us wants them in our service," spoke Ruapata. "What is to be done?"

"They must take an oath," Poneiva said. "As should any warriors of Hara'a who will not come into our service. Those who refuse, remain prisoner."

"Then it would be best you take them with you. I can not spare men to guard them." By that time, we were traveling toward the king's house. I found it surprisingly similar to that of Poneiva's family when we arrived, a rambling low place set among the fields. Ruapata was possibly no more wealthy or powerful than those vassals of Arierona.

We dined simply that night, the king and his closest advisers, Poneiva and myself. "We must not think Hara'a is defeated nor that he will not attack us again," Ruapata told us. "It is but a respite."

"But he may turn his attention elsewhere, my lord," said Ponei-va.

"Most certainly. My kingdom is not very important."

"Except as a way to the Teoma," the nobleman pointed out. "Arierona might be readily attacked from here."

The king nodded. I am sure he knew this. "Having failed to unseat me or raise my people against me, he may seek a different way. There is unrest in the lands of the High King himself, I hear."

"Lord Ruapata," I said, "There is unrest everywhere."

36. Ulani

"This young storyteller was at the house of the High King when I arrived," announced Heho, "and returned here with me."

Ulani smilingly greeted us. "Lady Pua sent me to her son. We are brothers now, after all." He pointed to a tatoo on his chest. "Ve'eta insisted I should get this to mark me as a member of his house."

I was just come from giving Ponu our report and already a messenger sped toward the house of the High King with all Poneiva and I had told him. Heho had been the one to bear news from the north to Arierona's nephew, only hours earlier.

Now he had brought Ulani to Rahaita and myself. "There is not much new to say of the situation in the north," Heho told us, as we sat in our greeting room. My son — *our* son — slept in the adjoining chamber. "Most of Mahutunoa's kingdom remains in the hands of the rebels. No man has been decided upon to take Revaru's place, though at least the fighting over that has seemed to settle down. And there is unrest in many places, even in Hei'iro's kingdom."

I knew the kingdoms of Va'aru, Arierona, and Avatu would be the most solidly against the rebels, the kingdoms along the Teoma, but even here one found dissension.

"It is good to hear there has been success here in the south, and that Hara'a —" At that moment, Aranu burst in, seeking word of his wife.

"Is all well in the north?" he asked Ulani. "Is Amirea well?

"She is, Friend Aranu," replied the storyteller. "She spends her days with Poa'ave — planning the arrival of their children." Ulani broke into a very wide grin.

"What, both of them?" asked my wife.

"It is so, Lady Rahaita."

Aranu seemed happily dazed and contributed little more to our conversation for a time. "It is likely they shall deliver within days of each other," continued Ulani. "Oorto is at hand if he is needed."

The boy sighed. "I did not wish to leave him, but he told me I must, that I was to be a great poet here in the land of my father. I think Oorto made that all up, for he is no foreteller, but I came. With a trader who knew Heho's secret path, I came."

"Did you finish your epic?" I asked. "Ve'eta would have wanted to hear it."

"And he did hear it, Taona. Three times. Oh, and he watched Lord Bafa's archers too. I think he wanted to learn to use a bow."

Lord Bafa. Yes, I suppose he would be called that now. The two had never met before, had they? Ulani's eyes flickered to Aranu and back to me. "Bafa loved Amirea once, did he not?"

"So did I, Ulani. That was long ago and in another world."

"Ah." Maybe he hoped for the makings of a story but I intended to give him no more. "And it was in this world she met her true love." I could see the cogs of creation moving about in his head; what Ulani did not know, he could make up.

Aranu broke his silence with a little laugh. "It is odd. I knew Amirea here at the house of Arierona and paid her no attention. It

161

was as if I had new eyes when I returned from across the mountains."

"You changed, my friend, as did she. You were both children a year ago."

"Yes," he agreed, "though I was a very large child!"

Ulani was called upon to repeat his epic here, too, as the household gathered to hear it. It proved a reasonably accurate account of our adventuring over the mountains and back, though as seen through the eyes of Oorto. I did feel at least a little uncomfortable being named over and over as a hero.

Aranu ate up similar descriptions of himself.

"Stay with us," invited Ponu. "We are honored to have such a teller of stories here." He slightly inclined his head, the ghost of a bow, in acknowledgment of Ulani's talent. "You reflect well on your master Isa."

"You knew the Taona Isa, Lord Ponu?" asked the young poet.

"He visited the house of Arierona more than once when I was a boy. The Taona lives yet, dwelling in the lands of the High King."

Ulani reflected on that for only a moment or two. "I should visit him."

"That would be proper," agreed the nobleman. "But return to us if you do."

The opportunity for that visit came within the week. "The High King has called for you, Marareta," Ponu told me. "He wishes to hear all there is to hear of your exploits in the kingdom of Ruapata." The request did not surprise me. Then he added, "And

Arierona thinks your counsel could be of help. Ve'eta admires you."

So I was again to leave Rahaita. "Pana'a told me we would be together," I grumbled to my wife, "yet we keep parting."

"But that has already come true. What might happen now is unseen."

"Unseen even to you?"

"A prophetess must be blind to her own fate. It is too difficult to look there."

I was willing to accept that. It even made a sort of sense. "I will leave Rika here. He and Hepetea can keep an eye out for what you can not see." Heho had already taken to the road again. Who besides Ulani might accompany me?

Aranu and Hito were who, but none of the men they commanded. Neither Arierona nor Ponu was willing to send more warriors north now. The two were given permission — or perhaps ordered — to travel with us. I did not ask which.

37. The Storyteller

In the southwestern corner of the High King's realm dwelt Isa, on a small river that flowed into the Teoma. Not that far, in fact, from the house of Arierona was his home.

We chose to cross over A'auwa as a start to our journey, quietly and without drawing attention, in a small canoe. In the still, dim hours of early morning that was, and the islands were hidden in mists. Then northward along the river we followed the pathway, less heavily traveled on this side of Teoma.

That, in part, was because of the many streams that were tributary. Some could be forded or even jumped over; the others we swam across. The land about us became lushly jungled. "This might be the stream," said Hito, as we reached yet another flow. Of us, he was by far the most familiar with this part of the Mora homeland — Aranu was born far away, Ulani even further, and I in another world. He went to ask a woman who stood watching with disinterest.

Satisfied with her answers, he returned. "The next one," Hito reported and dove into the waters.

The 'next one' proved somewhat broader. "We will have to cross sometime," said Ulani as we followed a narrow path by its flow, overhung with fruit trees. "I was told Isa's house was on the northern side."

That house, when we reached it, was more a hut. "Yes, travelers, that is the house of Taona Isa," we were told by an old man. He gazed over the river at the modest edifice. "You had best hurry across before he is too drunk." It was mid-afternoon. The ancient cackled, "I sometimes go over and help him with that!"

An easy swim — we dove into the dark shadowed waters. There were no dangers to be found in any waters in the Mora nation and the only crocodiles were those that preferred fish. I had wondered at our start whether Ulani would swim at all, having spent much of his youth in the dry savannas about the Diwarna trade town, but he must have learned at some point.

Possibly when he had been apprentice to the man we visited. That man came forth now and watched us pull ourselves out of the water and onto his dock. "I could have brought my canoe over to you," he called. "I welcome you — Ulani, is that you?" He came forward and embraced the dripping boy.

"Rania!" he called. "Come! It is Ulani." A slender woman, perhaps not quite middle-aged, came out to us, to likewise wrap her arms around young Ulani.

"My friends," said Ulani, presenting us. "Taona Marareta. Lord Aranu. Hito."

Isa peered at me and my tattoos. "A priest, eh? I welcome you as a friend of Ulani but I do not invite such here."

"The taona has little respect for the gods," whispered Ulani, as we followed the couple inside. "I am not sure he believes they exist."

The storyteller was not as old as I had been led to believe. There was undoubtedly a tendency to exaggerate those sorts of details. Perhaps sixty? Certainly not much more than that.

HERO FROM THE SEA

It was a spacious enough house, more than sufficient for this couple, one large room in the front, apparently two smaller chambers behind. Typical Mora construction was used, posts and crossbeams, with grass mat walls and thatched roof. We seated ourselves as Rania and, to our surprise, a servant, brought fruit and bowls of beer. The wife joined us as soon as we were served.

"The High King makes certain we get all we need here," she told us.

"More than we need," interjected Isa. "This new one — what's his name, my love?"

"Ve'eta, Husband."

"Yes, Ve'eta. He sends all sorts of things we do not need or want. It is wasteful!"

"Ve'eta appreciates story tellers," I said. "This I know is so." I looked to Ulani. "Your student just presented his new epic to him."

"You will have to give it to us too, my boy." I got the distinct feeling that the young poet would have preferred not. "But I have heard of this. Also that you were adopted into his family, which is no doubt a good thing." Isa did not sound so sure of it. "News does reach us here."

The rest of that afternoon and into the night Ulani told his tale, with no interruption for a meal, fresh sustenance being brought out from time to time. The Taona Isa would sometimes interrupt with a question, a suggestion, some small criticism. On whole, I believe he approved.

Then he looked at Aranu and me. "Are these the men of whom you tell?"

"They are, Taona."

"And also the foretold hero from the sea. I am skeptical of prophecies but here you sit, so I must believe." Isa shrugged and drank more beer.

"Do the gods truly speak to men, then?" asked Rania.

"We all know better here," I replied. Hito and Aranu had seen much of wizardry beyond the mountains and had a sense of what was involved. "It is a human gift, not a sending."

"That does not mean the gods do not speak, though, Taona," objected Hito. "Just that it is not quite as the priests have taught us."

"What else have they taught that is wrong?" asked Isa. "I believe nothing that comes from their mouths."

"We still honor many of the old ways in my father's home," spoke Aranu, softly. "And I still honor the priests. Especially this one." He nodded in my direction.

"I don't remember actually ever teaching anything," I replied.

"Yet I have learned much." There was no good answer to that one.

Both these young warriors tended be traditionalists, I realized, Aranu thanks to his rearing in the house of Hei'iro, Hito — maybe it was simply his nature. I knew him to be conservative, at least more so than most of his fellows. This is not to say he was in any way sympathetic to the rebels but, rather, that he favored the established order and was ambitious to rise within that order.

HERO FROM THE SEA

"You must remain with me a while," Isa told his former apprentice. "Need you journey on with your friends?"

Ulani looked to me and I shook my head. There was no need at all. "I would be honored to stay with you, Master."

"Good," said Isa. "Maybe we can fix the many problems with your epic."

38. Mahutunoa

Mahutunoa was one of the tallest Mora I had seen — not bulky like the huge Maitoa but perhaps topping him in height. He looked perpetually glum with his long, heavy-jawed face and, having lost a kingdom, had good reason to be.

He stood now beside the High King. "I wish Ulani had come with you," said that individual. "I wish I could get Isa to come here for that matter!"

We would gather Ulani on our return to the south. "I would rather that warriors had come with you," rumbled Mahutunoa. The king would most certainly have sung bass in any choir.

"We will get them," Ve'eta assured him. "We'll sweep the rebels before us!" He grinned. "Ulani has to be here to compose an epic about that. Anyway," he went on, "all the kings have pledged support."

"Pledging is not sending," noted Mahutunoa.

"My lord," spoke Arierona, "Hei'iro and I return to our kingdoms to gather our men. And this was good news we received of Ruapata." He looked toward me.

"Yes, yes," agreed the young High King. "My cousin Poneiva. He thrashed me once when we were boys." He looked slightly abashedly toward Arierona. "I was trying to steal honey from your hives."

Arierona could not help laughing. "So that was what that was about? Your mother told me someone had beaten you but you would not tell who."

Poneiva was, what, two or three years older than Ve'eta? "Indeed, Lord Arierona. I knew I was in the wrong." The High King looked out over the fields where warriors trained. Some of Bafa's bowmen were in one corner, having middling success at striking straw targets.

"I chafe for battle," he stated. "I let Heimanu hold me back far too long."

"The high priest is a long-winded old fool whose only concern is maintaining his own authority," stated Mahutunoa. He might owe the loss of his kingdom to the man.

Ve'eta nodded absently as he waved toward the archers and then gestured for someone to come join us. That someone was Bafa. "You will bring all your bowmen back with you, won't you?" he asked, giving Arierona a sidelong glance. They were the king's men, after all.

"Certainly, my lord. I've nearly a hundred more there. A hundred and one if I brought Teme." He gave me a wink.

"Good. I must train my men to use the bow. We shall be more than a ten hundred when we go to war at last. More than a twenty hundred!"

"Better twice even that number," remarked Arierona. "And we shall have them." Where was Hei'iro? I wondered. Preparing to depart? There was a contingent of his warriors here already, more than the eighty Arierona had brought. But a far greater number of men was needed, levies from all the kingdoms. Even Ruapata might spare a few warriors now.

But might not those better attack from the south? I was not a planner of strategy here but I was bound to think on such things.

Ah, here came the missing king, with his son. Aranu towered over his father and was certainly more pleasant of countenance. His looks must come from his mother — of whom, I realized, I knew nothing. But the fact that he was sent for his training to the house of Arierona suggested a relationship. Not important to me, who had no ambitions other than a peaceful life with the woman I loved.

"My lord Ve'eta, I shall depart in the morning," said Hei'iro. "At least two hundreds I shall send immediately to you."

"You will return?" asked the High King.

"That is my intention, but —" He looked a tad uncomfortable. "There is word of unrest in my own kingdom. I must make certain of its safety." Ve'eta nodded in understanding. He also understood that he could force none of the kings to send men.

"I too shall go," spoke Arierona. "And I promise as many. Including those bowmen you desire, my lord."

"That is good," said Ve'eta. "Avatu pledges to send men too, and Va'aru."

"What of Anana?" asked Mahutunoa, sounding as peevish as was possible for a man with his voice.

"He will meet us on the march. This he has promised." That made sense, considering where his kingdom lay. "What aid we will receive of Aritaku's scattered forces, who could say?" That noble had been named the official heir of Revaru — official in that he had the approval of the High King. Other warlords had their own claims on the kingship.

"I have more than five hundreds of my own warriors ready here," Ve'eta announced, "and more gathering. Nearly that many, too, of Mahutunoa's men escaped and are now with Anana. We have a good start."

Every man there, though, knew it was not nearly enough.

"I wish Hareata were here," Arierona whispered to me. "As does Hei'iro. I think those two formed some sort of alliance."

"Indeed," I replied, keeping my own voice low. "With Temani'i-tu. Where is the Lord Hareata?"

"Gone to meet with Va'aru and Avatu." A sensible use of the man's abilities.

"How many return, my lord?" I asked him.

"I wish to leave as many men as I can. Their officers are competent. I shall bring only two guards away with me and travel quietly south. Treat me," he said, looking into my face, "as another traveler."

"Bafa comes?"

"Yes, I wish him to get his archers ready." A quiet, throaty chuckle came and he looked down at the ground. "It is you two who draw attention. Especially Bafa who is lighter than you."

"As is Beka," I replied. "Won't he come too?"

"No, off with Hei'iro again."

"Oh." That was not too surprising. "If we stay east of the river, we may not be noted. We need to stop for Ulani anyway."

"Yes." The king nodded his head. "He will be needed to craft another epic before all this is over."

39. Taken

So it was the king and his two guards, Bafa, Aranu, Hito and myself who headed south. We looked ordinary enough, a small troop of warriors, obviously, headed somewhere on some business of our own. People did not tend to be particularly curious about such groups and there was enough rain to wear concealing ponchos part of the time.

Otherwise, the tattoos of a king would certainly have been a giveaway, more so than any light skin. I did not feel it necessary to remind Arierona of this.

It was overland to the river on which Isa dwelt, and then down its flow to his house. In this paradise of fruit and flower, of scented breeze and sweet bird song, it is not surprising we took few cautions.

Were they who struck even aware that a king walked with us? I was the target, the man who had been seen here a few days before. They had known we would return for our friend and that night, as my companions slept at the house of Isa, I stepped outside for no more important reason than to relieve myself in the prescribed spot (the Mora having many taboos about this activity which I have neither the time nor interest to enumerate).

Arms grasped me, many arms, strong arms. Something, some bark cloth I think, was stuffed into my mouth. In little more than seconds, I was bound and lying in a canoe, which was being vigorously paddled upstream. I could see by the faint light of the moon that these were not priests, nor ragtag rebels. These were warriors.

Where were they carrying me and to what purpose? The first question was perhaps not that difficult; they were almost certainly from the rebel force. Why they would want me was more puzzling. A day later we were on foot, I with my arms still bound and a tether preventing me from running. Running away, that is — we were all running toward the north with few stops for rest or nourishment.

I could have refused, of course, laid myself down and not moved, but I knew these men would not be gentle if I attempted such tricks. Better to go with them in as good a condition as possible.

Through largely uninhabited lands they led me, the savannas where few Mora lived. Eventually, my four kidnappers must have decided there was enough distance behind them. They settled onto the ground by a small stream, running between grass-grown banks, and motioned me to join them. "Eat, Man from the Sea," said one, handing me some leathery dried fish. Another brought a gourd of water from the brook. They all stared at me with some interest as I ate.

"He is a priest," remarked one. "That is the sign of Teva on him."

"That is no god for a hero," said another. "I do not understand what Hara'a wants with him."

"Not our concern, Brother," replied the first. "Let us sleep a few hours before going further."

A watch was set, not that I was likely to escape — I immediately fell into deep, exhausted slumber. The next day we again journeyed north. We met another party of warriors that day, and there was a conference involving much gesturing and pointing. At last, we set off again, but now traveled more westerly. I could only assume that our destination had changed. Or moved.

It was two days later that we reached the camp of the rebels, thousands strong. I was immediately taken to its center, where Hara'a stood speaking with his captains. I recognized the king, for I had seen him at the election of Ve'eta. As regal a man as anyone might imagine was Hara'a, tall, handsome, young. There was an air of arrogance in his bearing but that, perhaps, was a pose.

"The hero!" he exclaimed, on spying me. "At last you have come to me."

"I had little choice in the matter, my lord," I replied. My attempted smile was certainly a weary one.

"Yes, yes." Hara'a vigorously nodded his head. "We had to rescue you from those who would use you." So that was how he saw it. "The Hero from the Sea must help me bring back the old ways." And maybe put young Hara'a on the High King's dais?

I felt it best not to point out that another could be the prophesied hero. Indeed, had Bafa ventured out into the night, he might have been the one standing here. "I serve as best I can, Lord Hara'a." That was noncommittal enough.

"We will speak more of this later," said the king. "Now we march to battle." He turned to one of his commanders. "Aritaku's army is scattered then?"

"Yes, my lord. It is likely the king was slain, as well."

"He was no king," responded Hara'a. "Only a pretender." He pondered but a moment before giving his orders. "We march south. It is time to take the crown from Ve'eta's head." He smiled with decidedly blood-chilling nonchalance. "And to take Ve'eta's head from his body."

If I'd any doubts before, they were gone. This boy was quite mad. Soon all were on the march; I was unbound but surrounded by fighting men. Escape was no option for me.

That night, as we camped, the king called me again to him. "You are wed to the Lady Rahaita." It was a statement but I answered it anyway.

"That is so, my Lord Hara'a."

He went on, speaking almost as if in a trance. "I have seen her, shining as a star. She is a light in the great darkness." I began to suspect something. No, not suspect; this young man definitely had powers akin to those of Rahaita and Oorto. And as others before him, those powers had driven him to insanity.

"You have dreamed, my lord?"

"Yes. You understand! The gods speak to me. I can not escape their voices." I did understand and suddenly felt a great pity for the man. "As a boy, I slept near the Blood Stone, as I traveled with my father. That was when I first heard them. Now — now I am called to the Sacred Isle in A'auwa."

"It is a place of power," I allowed. "There are many."

Hara'a gazed into the night sky. "They are like a spider web hanging above the void, connecting all things. I am trapped in that web, Hero." I wished he would stop calling me that. He laughed. "I am but a hapless moth."

A moth or a spider? I wondered. But there was no need of metaphors to know that Hara'a was a great danger to the Mora people and to those I loved.

40. Victory and Defeat

Tahu glared. The lean, dark priest and his followers had joined Hara'a's warriors the previous night. It was obvious that he did not share the king's attitude toward me.

"Better you slay him, my lord," he hissed. "This man from the sea is not of our people."

"You had your chance at that," replied Hara'a, in quite reasonable tones. "You failed so it was not meant to be." That seemed logic enough for him.

But the rebel priest was not disinclined to speak to me, as we marched along. Perhaps as any villain in a melodrama, Tahu felt the need to explain himself. "Hara'a believes himself the tool of the gods," was his opening.

"Are not we all?" I answered. I could play the game of priests.

Tahu scowled and spoke no more.

So the troops of Aritaku had been defeated. From what I heard, they had been undisciplined and unready, and some nobles of his kingdom had joined the rebels against him. This was a great loss to the High King and those who followed him. Ve'eta could not be ready yet to take on this army of Hara'a. A few days more might be all that was necessary.

But the young High King did not wait for his promised reinforcements. Foolhardy, eager Ve'eta was marching toward us. Word was that troops of Anana were advancing also from the west.

And Hara'a himself also advanced. Battle should be joined within a day or two. I stood near the king as it came, on a clear and sunny morning, a morning better suited to song than the music of weapons. He had insisted I be ready at hand throughout our march.

"Anana's men have been turned at the Teiri," spoke a messenger who ran to the king, and crouched at his feet. "They do not come."

"Then the victory promised by the gods is ensured," said Hara'a. He looked at me. "There is a shrine of Te'eta near here. Take my guest there." Te'eta — the war god, the God of the Red Sky, the god whose priests carried knives of rose quartz.

It was to be those priests who guarded me, while warriors were about their business. That business could now be heard, distantly, as two armies met. Four priests. The warriors who had escorted me thrust me into a hut beside the shrine, where a crude stone likeness of the god stood, and hurried back to their war.

I was not bound. That was their first mistake. Perhaps Tahu's fanaticism prevented him from being as cautious as he should. Perhaps he did not see me as a warrior. I sometimes did not myself, yet I had been one often in this land. He set two of the priests to watch at some distance from the hut and then Tahu and his fellow crept upon me, rosy blades in their hands.

Here, Tahu indulged in neither explanations nor proclamations. He merely rushed forward with his knife. It would have been wiser not to get ahead of the other priest. I landed a solid blow to his midsection as he leaped and, for good measure, put a left hook into his crotch. The other priest hesitated. A mistake.

Then the fool came at me, another mistake. I had Tahu's blade in my hand by then, snatched up from where he had dropped it. A feint, a lunge, my shoulder into his chest and the knife into his gullet. He gasped and fell. Tahu rose, hurt and bewildered. Should I leave him behind me, alive? I decided that was a bad idea, and left him dead instead. To kill an unarmed man is not something of which one should be proud but he had just tried to murder me, after all. And for how many other deaths was he responsible? Let another figure out the morality; I acted and that was that.

Here came the other two priests running, only to see me with a bloody blade and two bodies at my feet. They fled from me. I, wisely I believe, quickly fled in the other direction. North I should go, to the hills. What was happening behind me, I did not know, but I suspected strongly that Hara'a and his men had the best of this battle.

Soon I was amid the tall grass and scrubby trees and expected no pursuit. Where to? I could not follow the trade road across the hills. It was certain to be watched and guarded. That there were other passes, some easier to traverse than others, I knew. Where they lay, I knew not. But these hills were not so high that one could not go over them anywhere, with enough effort. There were many steep places around which one must detour, the valleys were often choked with impenetrable brush, but ways could be found.

But I'd best not dawdle, with no food and no way to readily obtain it. One does not hunt successfully with a quartz sacrificial knife. Anyway, there was too much of a need to hurry for that.

HERO FROM THE SEA

I worked my up and along the gradual southern slope of the range. The hills rose more abruptly, often as cliffs, on their far side, but here I could make my way. Lowering myself down on the other side could be much trickier. Then — was that the trade road below me?

It had been closer than I realized and now I stood on a steep spot overlooking the pass. In fact, I realized, this was just the spot from which Alexander Nesmith had shot me a year earlier. I saw no men below. But if any were stationed there, they would be guarding the entrance, wouldn't they, not up here at the crest of the hills?

Best to be cautious, though. I waited until dark to slip through.

Less than three days later, I spied the trade village in the distance.

41. From Afar

"I have spoken from afar with Rahaita," Oorto informed me. "My news lifted a great burden. None knew what had become of you.

"I told her also of Hara'a. I have never felt him, nor has she, but we had not sought." He gazed thoughtfully into space for a moment, as though seeking the man then and there. "We may attempt that later."

Together. That would be wise. "Now I need to be thinking of getting home," I said.

"Not the way you came, I think," spoke Lady Pua. "One might or might not be able to make it through the kingdom of Anana."

I laughed. "That leaves only the Gurang."

"Indeed, Mika," said Oorto. They were serious. "Rahaita has already had a messenger dispatched to Temani'itu, asking that he send a vessel for you." He glanced at our companion. "And for Lady Pua."

"I need to be away from here," she said, quietly. "It is feared that my son is dead." I, too, feared this.

"It is not an easy way, my lady," I told her. But, on reflection, probably no harder than crossing over the hills. I turned to Oorto. "You will guide us?"

"I will. Now tell me of Ulani."

That I did, for some time. Then there was much catching up with those who had remained in this village, Gordie, the Nathans, even Amlee and Tala, who still lived and worked there. "We did not want to leave our cats, Taona," said Amlee. There were half-grown kittens about now, each appropriately named in Diwarna.

But the next day we began our journey. Gordie accompanied us, making four who traveled along the little stream that flowed north from that oasis in the savanna. Yes, his wife, Demba, was definitely pregnant, I had noted, as was Amirea. I hoped that Aranu could be reunited with her soon. I hoped that I could officiate their official Mora wedding.

It was not a difficult way and soon enough we reached a point where canoes awaited. As the Mora, the Diwarna had a habit of leaving their canoes in certain spots, for days, for weeks, nor did they greatly mind if some other found it necessary to borrow them while they were gone. Oorto and Gordie left a pair of canoes here regularly, as they passed back and forth from the trade town.

I too had passed back and forth on this route, but it had been long. Down the shallow river we paddled, the trees growing ever taller on each side, as we drew nearer the jungles of the Gurang. At last we reached that mighty flow.

"This is a very great river," marveled Pua. "I was told it was larger than the Teoma but never believed."

"There is a river beyond the mountains that outstrips this one," Oorto told her. The lengthy Tez — neither of us would see it and its great valley again, I was sure. There was no longer any need. In time, he and Gordie steered the canoes into the mazes of the swamps. Could our young sailor now find his way here as readily as the shaman who grew up among them?

A Diwarna village ahead, raised on piles. I knew it well, a common jumping off point for traffic to the trade village. It was here I had first met the brothers Maneata and Poneiva. Many canoes were drawn up to the docks below.

There on the platform, looking down at us, once again stood Poneiva.

Lady Pua was first to greet him. "How did you get here, young cousin? I see no Mora canoes."

"The Diwarna ferried me here," he called out, as we climbed the bamboo ladder to his position. "I have a larger canoe waiting in the river. Hail, Taona, and you too Oorto. Gordie. It has been long." It had indeed been long since he had last seen Gordie, who had returned to the Diwarna — and his Diwarna wife — shortly after our sortie against the Kohari.

"I went myself to Temani'itu, rather than send a runner," Poneiva continued, "as soon as the Lady Rahaita requested it. I beat you here only by hours." He turned to look soberly upon Pua.

"Any word of my son?" she asked him.

"It seems certain he was slain, my lady. It was a terrible defeat and his army was scattered." If only Ve'eta had waited. None of us would blame him now, though, whatever our thoughts might be. "As you have lost a son, so have I lost a friend," he softly spoke.

Lady Pua gazed steadily at the young man for some time. "You should be the High King," she said at last. "There is no other as worthy." I was rather inclined to agree, but none was likely to ask my opinion.

Poneiva did not seem surprised. "Ruapata has said the same to me," he admitted. "He intends to name me when the kings assemble." He half-smiled and shrugged. "It seems an unlikely role for me."

"Arierona will surely back you," I said, "but not if we remain here." So no sooner had we arrived than we departed, descending to the dock and back into the canoes of Oorto and Gordie, with one more passenger now.

Through the swamps we threaded, heading, I was fairly certain, a bit west of north rather than following the way by which we had come. A couple hours later we reached the main flow of the great Gurang.

I should not have been surprised that we came to the river precisely where Poneiva's canoe lay. It was a larger vessel, with outrigger and tall mast, and two Mora waited for us upon it. Pua and I boarded, Poneiva behind us.

Oorto held up a hand in farewell. "Voyage safely, Friend Mika. Your wife will learn that you come." He and Gordie turned their canoes and paddled back into the tangled trees, quickly disappearing from our view.

Poneiva handed me a paddle. "Let us be on our way."

42. Full Circle

"Traders," said Poneiva. "No need to worry."

A rather large Kohari vessel was moored close to the shore. Not that the Gurang actually had a shore here, its waters disappearing amid the trees. We were still upstream from the mangrove morass of the coast, still where the tall jungle trees shaded the river. The Mora paddled over to the boat; there a pair of Kohari lounged, looking over the railing at us.

"Ho, Man from the Sea!" called one of them. I could not have put a name to him but he was one I had met and drank with below the Great Falls.

"Hail, Friend," I returned. "We have both traveled far since last meeting."

My ease with the Kohari was not something my companions might have expected. "That we have," he replied. "We come for lumber to take back to your people."

"You are cutting trees?" called Poneiva.

"We've picked a likely one over there." The man gestured vaguely upstream. "You should take a look. You Mora could make a very fine large canoe of it."

"We have no time, sir," Poneiva responded. "I'll have to wait until you bring it back to Temani'itu."

"You cut logs for the Mora?" I asked. "I did not know this."

"The Mora tolerate our presence on the Gurang if we bring logs down for them. The priests and chieftains at home do not like this but know it is best not to interfere." The Kohari winked. "Not that we would let them. And then we trade also with those who live here, those you name the Diwarna."

I wondered briefly how these stone age people toppled the huge trees. There might be some other time to learn of that; now, we needed to resume our journey. The Gurang grew very broad but also broke into channels, running to the sea through the mangrove. The water was only slightly brackish, for the river's flow was voluminous and this was a coast without much in the way of tides.

The triangular mat sail was raised and we set a course to the south. The winds seemed fickle, the journey to take longer than we wished. But it was perhaps not that long, truly, but only we who were impatient.

Ahurataca rose before us, as it eventually must. "I shall stop for any news," called Poneiva from his place at the stern. This canoe was not too large to bring close in to the beach, though running it onto the sand would add an unnecessary delay. As we drew near, Poneiva dove into the surf and swam ashore, in the cove I had visited only weeks earlier.

It seemed deserted. Were there not usually men and women busy on this beach? Fishermen used it, and there should be guards atop the cliff, lookouts posted on order of the High King. It would be madness to not guard the cliffs surrounding the Mora homeland.

We saw Poneiva go to the cliff and gaze upward. No rope was lowered for him. After a few moments, he returned to the water and swam out through the waves to us. "No one is there," he reported, "save for one dead man below the cliffs. The sun and the gulls have left nothing to recognize him by."

"If a Kohari war party found it like this, our people would be in great danger," said one his men.

"They are already in great danger," Pua told him

Further along the coast, however, men could be seen at their posts atop the cliffs, and canoes came and went from the coves and small harbors. We waved but did not again stop. Our need to reach the Great Falls and the way home seemed too urgent now.

Finally, we rounded a point to behold the wide bay where Teoma dropped over several cliffs to the sea. The Great Falls lay before us. Poneiva steered our canoe onto the beach and many hands helped pull it well up on the sand.

"We have watched for you, Lord Poneiva," reported one man. "Yes, and your brother waits here with Temani'itu," another told him. Then a third recognized Pua. "Lady Pua," he whispered hoarsely. "Our welcome to you." The group became far less exuberant, knowing of her loss. To the house of all who sail on the sea we went.

I had traveled a great circle over the past few weeks, to find myself back here. Lord Temani'itu came forth and embraced his sister tenderly, and then greeted each of us in turn. "Your brother is lazing somewhere," he told Poneiva. "Maybe fishing again."

Of the situation at Ahurataca we told him, as food and drink were brought. We had settled onto mats on the sand, before the long, low hut. "As he who watches the coasts, I must attend to this," he decided. "I shall send men to watch from below immediately. Those atop the cliffs," Temani'itu said, "serve the High King and Anana. I can only guess that enemy warriors slew those who watched there." He shook his massive head. "Such a thing is unheard of!"

He spoke then to Lady Pua. "What is to be done now? No other nephew of Maitoa has the age to become High King and the cousins —" His distaste for those was obvious.

"You think only of the first cousins, Brother," she replied. "We have a much better cousin right here drinking your beer."

Temani'itu raised his eyes to peer at Poneiva. "He might do," he rumbled. "Better than me having to take the job anyway." He turned his attention back to his meal.

I was pretty sure that meant he supported my friend. Men would listen to Temani'itu.

"This oaf as High King?" came a voice from the shadows. "My parrot can carry on a more intelligent conversation." Beka came and plopped down beside his brother. There was, in fact, a parrot on his shoulder, a bird mostly green and yellow of feather.

It squawked something in what was almost certainly Kohari. I could guess where he had obtained the bird.

"I thought you would be with Hei'iro," I said.

"I chose to remain here rather than travel again to his house, Marareta. It is a very dull place to spend time."

"That it is," agreed Temani'itu. "I spent a week there once. It was the most miserable month of my life." He belched and wiped the beer from his mouth with the back of a ham-sized hand. "He and the other kings will be gathering up there." He nodded toward the cliffs. "I suppose I shall have to go back myself."

The parrot interrupted with a loud and obscene expletive.

"Exactly," said the admiral.

43. Leaders

"I always wanted a parrot," explained Beka, "even when I was sailing the Great Lakes."

"From the jungles of darkest Ohio, no doubt."

Our companion had no idea where those places were. Nor, I think, did he care. "You don't for a moment believe Miruhata will let you keep that, do you?" asked Poneiva.

"Give it to Teme," I suggested.

"She might teach it even worse language than it already knows," Beka said. "You know what a temper she has, Brother."

"That I do," affirmed Poneiva.

"You know," I said to the pair, "if Poneiva does somehow find himself on the High King's dais, Teme's sons will be seen as likely successors."

Beka thought on that. "She would be like the new Lady Pua!"

That we all had to laugh about. The original Lady Pua remained with her brother, both to follow us sometime later — a day, maybe two. We had already clambered to the top of the cliffs and followed now the road to Lake Aedina. This time, one of us did know the location of that mysterious bridge Aranu had sought; Beka led us off the main path and down to a distressingly long suspension bridge high above the churning waters of Teoma.

"I crossed here on my way down to the beach," he told us. "Nothing to it."

"Do you think it can hold all three of us at once?" Poneiva whispered to me. I thought it likely, but wished this pair weren't heavyweights. Poneiva easily weighed half again what I did, and Beka not much less.

And it swayed, that bridge did, like a ship in a rolling surf, like the hips of a Mora dancer. I fixed my eyes on the far side and eventually reached it.

From there, a narrow and lightly traveled pathway led to the house of Va'aru. It was rather scenic from this side, much closer to the river and the lower falls that lay just below Aedina. A stairway cut from the rock took us finally to stand beside the lake.

There was no Va'aru at his house. There was, however, Lord Hareata. "I have been finding places for those fleeing the war. It is known that Hara'a is advancing toward the house of the High King."

"But there is no High King," I said.

"No. A new one will be chosen in time. Names have been whispered." He glanced toward Poneiva. "It is certain now that Ve'eta fell. Aritaku as well. There, too, a new king must be chosen."

The nobleman sighed deeply. "It is known that the son of Pua fought well and died well. This we have of Mahutunoa, who was with him."

"Then he survived yet another lost battle?" asked Poneiva.

"That he did, and then pulled together the remnants of Ve'eta's army and marched to the aid of Anana. They threw back the force invading that kingdom and no rebels are now west of the Teiri.

"There will again be men guarding the cliffs," he added. That watch was a sacred duty to most Mora and the slaying of the lookouts was a great crime. If the concept were known here, it would have been a sin as well.

"Now Anana and Mahutunoa draw more warriors to themselves, and Va'are and Avatu camp with their forces near the house of the High King. Arierona and Hei'iro have sent men and are said to be on their way." He looked about before proceeding and whispered. "There was an uprising in the kingdom of Hei'iro. The king put it down but it is best not gossiped about."

"Who commands, then?" I asked. It seemed the logical question.

"The kings pledge to follow Temani'itu for now, whether he desires to lead or no." But he could not lead them into battle. A general would have to be chosen, probably one of the kings. "I shall wait here for him and Lady Pua."

Ruapata, apparently, remained in the south. It made sense for the king to stay there on Hara'a's flank, even if he had not enough forces to attack him. Ponu, too, kept guard at the house of Arierona.

We lingered only hours in that house by Aedina. My desire was to return to Rahaita, and Beka certainly would not have minded ending his long absence from Miruhata. Poneiva, however, was for going to the army of Va'aru and Avatu. It was on our way, or almost, so we acquiesced. Up Teoma we paddled, and turned at the Teiri. It was not much further to the camp of the kings.

On the banks of the river they had assembled. How many thousands I could not say; two or three, perhaps? And more promised by Arierona and Hei'iro. The first thing to catch my eye was the contingent of bowmen, a little separate from the other warriors. Was Bafa with them? It seemed to be his full troop.

But first, we must present ourselves to the leaders. The three of us — or four, if we counted the parrot — were pointed in the proper direction. Beka, incidentally, informed us that the parrot's name was Palala, a Kohari word meaning something like 'lucky.' "It was the name that decided me," He said. "I figured I could use some luck."

"As long as it is not double lucky," I answered, that being the name of J.L. Nathan's ill-fated yacht. Poneiva could not understand why we found that so humorous.

Va'aru sat in the shade of a palm frond lean-to, listening to a messenger who knelt nearby. The gray haired man beside him I recognized as Avatu. That individual had reigned long in the peaceful and prosperous lower valley of the Teoma, longer than any of his fellow kings. He had never been one who sought to upset things.

We were motioned to seat ourselves. Outside the shade, unfortunately. In time, the two kings turned their attention to us. We gave our story, I from the time I was kidnapped by the rebels. "So you were at the battle," mused Va'aru.

"Not quite, my lord," I answered. "Near the battle would be more accurate."

He nodded. "We met many warriors as we advanced, fleeing that battle. Those are now among our own men. Knowing of the disaster before us, we felt it best to fall back to here and await reinforcements."

HERO FROM THE SEA

"I am gladdened to hear that you disposed of Tahu," spoke Avatu. "And with his own blade — that is fitting." That blade had been thrown aside, soon after crossing the northern hills. I had no need of souvenirs.

"But we shall make more use of you, all of you," said Va'aru, who then slowly smiled. "And now we have all three of those who might be the Hero from the Sea with us. We must learn which it is!"

44. One to Speak

This new king was named as his late uncle, Revaru. Whether the nobles of his own homeland supported him was, at best, questionable, but the other kings had agreed to recognize the youth. No more than sixteen, I guessed, and unlikely to be of consequence in the coming struggle.

He chose to attach himself to us. Maybe no one else was paying any attention to him or maybe it was a case of hero worship.

Two days after our arrival, Hareata came. "Temani'itu and the Lady Pua rest at your house, Cousin," he told Va'aru. "They saw no reason to go further."

"Then who will command here?" asked Avatu.

"That leader the kings may choose. Yet Lord Temani'itu has chosen one to speak for him." He paused, letting that sink in before giving a name. "That one is his noble cousin, Poneiva."

Not to lead, but to have a voice, to counsel. And to speak with the voice of Temani'itu; it was a good balance between giving too much power to the young warrior, creating resentment, and too little, leading to him being dismissed. Hareata undoubtedly had a hand in crafting it.

Now Poneiva was called to the attention of all, and some would remember that he journeyed from an ancient house, even as spoken of in the prophecy, and that his destiny had been entwined with those of the supposed heroes from the start.

"This is acceptable to me," spoke Avatu.

Va'ru nodded. "Even Hei'iro might not object too loudly." Hei'iro was only a day away with his army, ferrying them across the Teoma even now. Arierona's force camped to the south, to advance separately when the time came. It was to be hoped that the men now in Anana's kingdom would also be prepared to do this.

Hei'iro in fact arrived within hours, coming with the vanguard while his men continued to cross the river. He did no more than shrug when he heard of Poneiva. "Is my son here?" he asked.

With Arierona, he was told. Aranu had his duties as the commander of a hundred. That might seem a fairly lowly position for the son of a king, even one so young, but that hundred was the king's personal guard. The boy would be close to Arierona's side.

I myself had no duties in this camp nor any other. Advice I could give and it might be no worse than another's. My position once we marched was just as uncertain. I thought I might do well to stay near Bafa and his archers. Had I not stood protection for the boy in our last great battle together, at the time of the Kohari invasion?

Indeed, there should be a force of men with just that task, to protect the bowmen. As we sat at our evening meal, I mentioned it to Poneiva and Beka. We three ate together when we could — I think Poneiva felt it a good way to get my informal opinion on this and that.

"You and Beka should lead it," said Poneiva. "There are men here who can be assigned." Those warriors sent earlier by King Arierona were recognized as being under Poeneiva's direct command. They were not numerous, but it prevented him from being a leader without followers.

"That will put all three of us so-called heroes in one spot," Beka pointed out.

"Which might not be a bad thing," his brother thought. "But I may need one or the other of you closer to me when battle comes."

This I told to Bafa in the morning. "We'll be marching in a day or so, won't we?" he asked.

"It would seem so. Our general is here." Hei'iro had been recognized by the other kings as best suited to that role. "We only await the rest of his troops."

"It is rumored that the rebels burnt the house of the High King to the ground." He stared out across the camp, at nothing in particular.

I had heard this. "I do not know. If so, they are close."

"Or some of them." That was true. Hara'a's main army might not have advanced so far. Indeed, it could have been a local uprising, if it happened at all. "I am eager to have my archers tested," Bafa went on, "but not so much to have any of them killed. Or anyone killed, Marareta."

"As the son of a king, that is going to be part of your life." It was an inescapable truth.

"Quite so," he agreed, rather absently. "Marriage will too. Arierona keeps suggesting matches."

I couldn't help having Teme come to mind, and a smirk come to my face. But I said nothing.

I did not need to. "Oh, I know well that little Teme has set her cap for me. She's not the first, after all." There was some of the old George Bath I remembered. He grinned at me. "The girl told me of the pact you two once made."

"Maybe you should do the same."

"Maybe so. In three years — well, I may not live beyond three days, so no point in thinking about that now!"

"Young Revaru would be a better match for her," I mused. The young king was standing not far away, trying to learn how to handle a bow from one of Bafa's men. He kept following me places.

"He may have only three days as well," Bafa reminded me. "His troops are going to be joined to ours, aren't they?"

I nodded. "Under Poneiva's command, yes. There aren't many, little more than the boy's bodyguards, I think." But there were a good number of warriors from his kingdom with Anana's army. Whether those men would recognize Revaru as their king when all this was over and we were victorious, who could know?

Victorious? Yes. Hadn't the prophecies said as much? And I know one must take care in the interpretation of prophecy, but the Hero from the Sea *would* give all the land its king.

45. Gifts

"Arierona is here," Beka told me. As he spent much of his time with his brother, he generally knew what was going on. I figured I would learn things soon enough.

"With his men?" That was not the plan.

"No, only a small guard. He wishes to confer now that Hei'iro has arrived."

This would be it, the final meeting before we marched against Hara'a. I was always welcome in those meetings, despite having no authority here. 'Hero' was apparently enough to gain me entry.

I hurried to where the kings and commanders stood. Was Arierona addressing them? He glanced in my direction and nodded. The king had, for some reason, been awaiting my arrival.

He beckoned me. "Come, my son." That 'son' thing again. "This pertains also to you." To Poneiva he turned. "This weapon was brought to me by the Taona Marareta from the land beyond the mountains. I give it now to you, Lord Poneiva, to carry further."

"To carry into battle!" He presented the sword-like bronze club to the warrior.

I was certainly not insulted nor bothered by this. Passing gifts on to another was rather common among the Mora, a way to further entangle their webs of obligation. In their eyes, both I and Arierona gave the club to Poneiva.

And I hoped he liked it. Poneiva would be able to handle its weight, that was for sure. I watched him go through a few movements common to the use of the weapon. He seemed satisfied with how it handled.

Arierona spoke again to the group. "I shall depart now to meet my army as it advances and yours as it attacks!" He immediately turned and walked away, followed by a few guards, through and out of the camp.

"We too shall leave in the morning," announced Hei'iro. "All make ready!"

Meeting adjourned, apparently.

I found myself wondering where Heho was. I had not seen the courier in a while; no doubt he traveled the road to somewhere or another, carrying the words of other men. He was too valuable in that role to join us in battle.

Were he here now, I would give him some of those words, some of mine, to carry south to my wife.

"Taona."

I turned; it was Hareata. "Lord Hareata. Are you ready to march?"

He shook his head. "I am asked to remain, to be here if the battle does not go well. It is something that must be considered. If all fails, we can turn to Lord Temani'itu. Others have sailed away into exile in our people's past." I wondered to what lands they had sailed. Were there other Mora settlements somewhere in this world?

"I think maybe our own ancestors, those nine canoes, were such refugees." He looked to where Poneiva was again going through some moves with his new club, while a handful of men looked on.

"I should speak to the Lord Poneiva before leaving. May the gods smile on you, Hero."

The two greeted and walked away, conversing of something. I walked the other direction, so I know not how long they spoke. Poneiva I did not see again until morning. By that time, the warriors were being formed into their troops for our march north, thousands of well-trained, determined Mora, with spears and clubs, shark-tooth swords, stone axes and, yes, nearly a hundred long bows.

Poneiva carried his new club, his gift. When he fought, it would be tethered to his wrist — as would my own wooden club — but now it hung across his back. Very visible there, as might have been intended.

"To me," he called, motioning to Bafa and me. Beka stood beside him already.

"Walk with me as we begin our march. Hareata says this will look good — the three Heroes from the Sea going forth to battle with me."

We looked at one another and all four burst into laughter.

Then we and an army marched forth.

Part IV. A Hero Comes

46. Destruction

There was a head atop a post. Our leaders paused a moment to look at it and marched on.

"Do you know who it is?" whispered Bafa, as we drew near.

"Heimanu," I answered. "The high priest." Yes, that was Heimanu, the old hypocrite, his eyes now staring into nothingness. For all his faults, he did not deserve this. Did anyone?

"Why would he have stayed?" my companion wondered. "Did he believe he could be on both sides at once?"

"Perhaps." We passed on by. One could not be neutral in a conflict like this, a war driven by fanaticism. Not even the high priest of all the Mora.

Yet fanaticism, too, had its roots. It did not spring up without reason, but must reflect deeper problems in the Mora society. It was not by chance that these rebels were strongest in the poorest parts of the land, not the rich Teoma valley. I realized that it would be hopeless attempting to explain this to most Mora. Lord Temani'itu, I think, saw some of it. Maybe Hareata did but he was too invested in the philosophy of his party, their reforms and modernization. It was all well to sweep away taboos but not the traditions that held together a society.

HERO FROM THE SEA

Enough of that. Maybe these problems would work themselves out peaceably in time; maybe it would take violent revolution. Right now, I knew what side I was on and whom I was protecting.

We marched not far behind the kings who were, in turn, just behind our vanguard. Out of respect, the three older monarchs allowed young Revaru to be with them, but he would regularly drop back to walk with us for a time. When battle approached, both Va'aru and Avatu would go to their own troops; best they be seen then by their men, even if they left command to others. Revaru would be with us, for his small band of warriors was joined to that Poneiva commanded.

The house of the High King had indeed been burnt, his gardens destroyed, but of the rebels' army there was no sign. The main force had not advanced so far. It would not be sensible for Hara'a to extend himself now, with Anana's army still a threat, ready to take advantage. He would let us come to him.

Warriors were not responsible for this wanton destruction, the burning of not only the High King's house but every building around it, to the least hut or pig sty. Bodies there were too, servants butchered for no seeming reason. This was insurrection of the bloodiest sort, driven by hatred, fanned by fanaticism.

Though Hara'a may have had no direct hand in it, these were still his crimes. He had brought this war to the homeland of the Mora, sought to use the rebels for his own ends. How long had the king plotted such a course? Perhaps since first he thought he heard gods speaking to him.

So on we marched to face him. Marched? That suggests order. There was little order to a Mora army on the move. Most kept to their own groups and those groups remained in more-or-less the proper position. But there were no disciplined columns of soldiers, nor any reason for them.

Until now, perhaps. The introduction of bowmen called for formations that had not previously existed. Would these people now follow the bloody path to more modern military tactics? Would this inevitably lead to the phalanx, to the knight, to the musket and the machine gun? Human progress, for better or worse, progresses.

Those ahead halted and the army predictably bunched up, some, although the call to stop echoed back through the troops. Men were being dispatched here and there, and Avatu and Va'aru hurried away to their troops. I doubted that Hara'a was particularly near, not over the next hill, just close enough that it was time to ready ourselves for battle in a day, or in two.

Young Revaru came to us. "We're going to fight now!" He swung his flint-edged sword about in an eager and somewhat dangerous manner. The teen-aged king was not small — as tall as me, in fact, and undoubtedly heavier — and like most nobles had been trained well in weapons. Which was good, as no one would be able to watch over him if he chose to plunge into the battle.

Poneiva's command, our mix of warriors from more than one kingdom, our archers, was to move forward and advance in parallel and to the left of Hei'iro's men, who now moved up to join their king. These had been marching along right behind us until this point. Va'aru and Avatu shifted their men toward the flanks. That was about as far as planned tactics went.

Strategy was even sketchier. There were surely messengers flying to both Anana to the west and Arierona on our right. It was time for the forces of Anana and Mahutunoa to cross the Teiri. Counting their army and that of Arierona, our numbers would increase by more than half. That would put us on a more even footing with Hara'a.

It was also time for men to prepare themselves, even as they marched along. Weapons and shields were unslung. Rudimentary armor was donned by those who favored such, made of crocodile hide or shark skin or tough woven fiber. Many Mora disdained such and fought nearly naked. I saw helmets of leather and crocodile teeth, and ones of feathers that offered no physical protection but promised spiritual aid. Petitions to a very large number of gods were also being delivered in a cacophony of prayer.

Possibly, as a priest, I too should have prayed, or blessed my troop, even as other priests were doing throughout the army. But how does one petition a god of love and rain before joining battle? It seemed more than a bit blasphemous. No, Teva was a god for home, for peace, for family, a god who watched over loved ones and brought rain for the crops. He did not belong here.

I felt that I did not either, but it was too late to do anything about that. So I mumbled something about asking the favor of all the gods for the sake of those near enough to hear me and prepared to fight.

47. Battle Joined

A stone went whizzing uncomfortably close to my head. Hara'a's men might not have bows but they did have slings. That was a weapon of the commoners, of farm workers and laborers, but every bit as deadly as those carried by noble warriors.

Our armies had drawn close near nightfall and neither chose to attack, other than a bit of harrying here and there by raiding parties. The main bodies sat and watched each other, encamped in the open rolling country beyond the northern borders of the High King's realm. It might have been better for Hara'a to throw his men against us then and there, before Anana and Arierona could reach us.

Perhaps he feared they would arrive after battle was joined and attack his flanks under cover of darkness. And perhaps he thought himself strong enough that he could overthrow us anyway. Attack came with day.

I am not sure which side first advanced. Both were ready when the sky began to lighten, and the priests of Te'eta could be heard chanting in the enemy camp, greeting the coming of the Red Sky. There were priests of Te'eta in our camp, too, and they were just as certain of their god's favor.

I half-wished that Teva would send a downpour and we'd all call this affair off. But Teva didn't do that, did he? There were storm gods for that sort of thing. Too late to ask for a typhoon. Surely those took some planning.

HERO FROM THE SEA

The archers were positioned, and released volley after volley of arrows into the thickly-packed opposing army. I and my men stood about them, to protect if any reached us. Though it went against Mora nature, Bafa and I were quite prepared to fall back with our force if pressed. We could do more good — or harm, depending on where one stood — from a distance.

The rest of our force, men of Arierona and Mahutunoa and Revaru, charged forward to engage the enemy, as did those of Hei'iro to our right and Avatu on the left. Beka was in the forefront of the charge, and young Revaru did not hesitate to rush forward with the others, here on land that was a part of his own war-torn kingdom.

Poneiva did not rush but stood with us; he was a leader now and could not indulge himself. Not immediately. Someone needed to give orders, to receive orders, though as the two masses of men met in chaotic struggle, few orders were likely to be heard or obeyed. Now the troops of Arierona were here and drove into the rebel left; not enough to shift the battle. Soon, they were engaged in the same warrior-to-warrior combat as the rest.

"There is no reason to stay here longer," stated Poneiva, and joined the fight. We continued to send our missiles arcing over the battlefield but could no longer pick targets in the melee. It was only possible to drop arrows toward the rear, where our side had not penetrated, and hope they struck someone.

Hara'a's men were pushed back there some, on our right. They advanced some to our left. A breakthrough at the middle — no, there was Poneiva himself, leading the warriors who pushed them back, his brother Beka at his side. Beka was making a good bid for being the Hero from the Sea on this day. I could see Poneiva's bronze club flashing in the morning light.

"Hold!" shouted Bafa, raising a hand. His archers lowered their bows. "No sense in wasting more arrows now. We shall wait and see where those we have left will be most useful," he told me. Bafa surveyed the troop. "The men are eager to throw down their bows and join the fight."

"It chafes a Mora warrior to stand and watch a battle," I said.

"It chafes me a tad," he replied. "Ah, look!" It was the force of Mahutunoa and Anana, advancing toward the enemy's right flank. "They'll try to come from behind," he opined.

"Fewer than hoped for," was all I could say. "We could try to create some confusion over there to help the attack."

"Excellent idea, old boy." Even in Mora, he was able to say things like that. We rapidly moved ourselves a good distance toward the west and took up a new stance. "This hill was put here just for this purpose," exclaimed Bafa, positioning his bowmen.

Soon they were dropping the remainder of their arrows into the men Anana was charging. The two forces met and we could no longer shoot. Not that it mattered — the arrow supply was all but depleted. Bafa turned to his erstwhile archers. "Shall we attack?" he called to them. A roar of approval met the suggestion, as men dropped their bows to grasp axes and clubs. He and I, archers and guards, charged down the hill to join battle.

HERO FROM THE SEA

We were met fiercely. A section of Hara'a's right flank had swept around, away from the attack by Anana, and was attempting to get behind Avatu's warriors. We were now blocking them.

Our one advantage was that we were the freshest men on the battlefield, having been held away from the fighting until then. Our disadvantage was that we were somewhat outnumbered by the advancing warriors, and could expect no assistance from Avatu's harried men. A massive assault had been thrown against their front for just this reason, so an attack might swing around behind them without challenge.

But in drawing men away from their own center to attack Avatu, the rebels gave Poneiva's men breathing space, even as we were being pushed back, inexorably. A tall Mora warrior pressed me, bashing at my shield with his heavy axe. How much longer could my already numb arm deflect such attacks?

Then the turmoil of battle separated us and I faced new opponents. All around me, our men battled the rebel force, spear against spear, club against club, falling, giving ground, but fighting on. The attackers were trying to slip around to our right, to carry through with their planned assault on the loyalist rear.

Into that gap charged Poneiva and his fighters, shouting war cries, to block their way.

48. Battle Abandoned

Block the advance, they did. This was far from being all of Poneiva's command, which battled on still further to our east, young Revaru among them, but it was more than enough to break their front. The enemy sortie fell back to regroup, as both our forces came together, prepared to drive a wedge through their ranks. Poneiva, wielding his bronze club, was at the point of that wedge, and Beka and Bafa and I flanked him, our own weapons at ready.

I — and Bafa, I am sure — will readily admit that Beka and Poneiva were much more effective in the hand to hand combat than we were. The two of us were similarly armed, with the Mora club, a flattened piece of hardwood handled somewhat like a sword. Bafa had studied fencing in the world from which we came, so it was an obvious choice for him. Beka preferred to employ the heavy ax his brother had carried until recently, its polished green stone head rising and falling as he forced his way forward. The attackers retreated before us to rejoin their main force.

This was just the show they wanted, wasn't it? Poneiva and the three Heroes pushing back the enemy, saving the day and maybe everything else.

Push them back we did. Then they pushed us back. The fight continued.

But then, on both sides, conch horns were being blown, men were being called back to reform their ranks. Slowly, the fighters disengaged, battle was abandoned, and warriors glared at each other from a distance, too weary now to shout challenges and insults. Anana and Mahutunoa brought their men around to join our main body. Would we again hurl ourselves against each other?

The sun already stood past its zenith and both armies seemed too exhausted to initiate another attack. We still seemed evenly matched. There was no easy victory ahead.

"We have not won this day, but we have stopped Hara'a," stated Hei'iro to the commanders. "I would wager he will not attempt to advance further." Being Mora and great gamblers, they asked for odds.

A man came forth from the rebel army, hands held high, and called to our leaders. "Lord Hara'a asks we fight no more today but tend to those who lie fallen." A moment's discussion, then a reply. "It will be so."

Hundreds lay dead or wounded, men of both armies. All together they lay, tangled, and who might say which lord they had followed at the start of this day? With the dead, it did not matter. Warriors of both sides carried them to lie together, equally honored — even the rebel commoners. Had they not fought, too?

Those not too badly wounded could tell whom they served; those nearer death were mercifully dispatched. That was the way of the Mora warrior.

Neither side seemed eager to renew the attack. Perhaps the leaders on both sides knew it was pointless. Maybe the men who served them knew it as well. As the sun slid westward, we could see the opposing force cautiously preparing to withdraw. "Will we pursue?" asked an eager Revaru. "Could we attack now and finish them off?"

"I think not," Poneiva answered him. "Not with no clear advantage and night coming."

Hei'iro and the other commanders apparently felt the same way. They would not risk an attack. For now, the enemy was crippled and driven back, but not broken.

That night, our army sat about its camp fires, resting, conversing in hushed tones of the day's events. There were no answering fires from the enemy camp. They were obviously withdrawing under cover of darkness.

In those conversations, one name appeared frequently and that was Poneiva. In the circles of the warriors, warriors from all the kingdoms of the Mora, it was whispered. By the fires of the kings and commanders, thought was given to the prophecies and how the young nobleman from the south might fit them. His courage on the field was remembered, and his leadership.

And his companions — we too were spoken of. There was much debating over which might be the Hero from the Sea. I did not care. I had seen too much of battle, here and elsewhere in this world. I envied Rika, still at the house of Arierona with his wife. Would I were with mine!

Hito found his way to me that night, and sat for a while by the fire. He had quit that house not so long ago himself, with Aranu and King Arierona. "The Lady Rahaita was well when we departed, Taona," he informed me. "Rika is growing fat and lazy while his wife spoils him." I suspected Hito was still on the search for a similar woman to spoil him.

"How fared Aranu and your troop this day?" I asked him.

"Some lived, some died." The warrior shrugged. "That is the way of battles." He paused for a few seconds to gaze into the flames. "It is not good for Mora to slay Mora.

"Aranu took a few small wounds," he continued. "He is one to throw himself on the enemy and hope his men follow him."

"He needs to remember that he, too, has a wife to whom he should return," I remarked.

Hito nodded. "Beyond the hills." He glanced northward toward those hills and then to me. "The way there may be opened again now. I think our friend Oorto has, what, spoken to your wife from afar? Is spoken the right word?"

"As good as any for we who do not understand it. Did she send any message for me?"

"No, Taona. The lady said nothing of it to me. I learned of this from Rika and he from Hepetea." His wife — she served Rahaita now.

"So be it. Nothing to do now but wait to see what tomorrow brings," I said, "and share the little beer I have left."

What the next morning brought was a scout's report. "Hara'a has passed north of the Teiri," he told the kings. Here, that river flowed more east to west, after turning at Marihana.

"Then he still occupies my lands," stated Mahutunoa. It remained unspoken that many of the king's people had supported this revolt. Even if Hara'a removed his army, it might not be easy to restore Mahutunoa to his kingdom.

Hei'iro stood gazing northward, towards the vanished enemy's position, shifting his weight from foot to foot. "So what action should we pursue?" he asked of the others.

"We should secure the road through the hills," Anana stated. This action would also help secure his own eastern border.

"That's a start," agreed Mahutunoa. "At least the western end of my kingdom could be freed from these rebels."

Our commander nodded. "Then you two should take your force north and do this. We shall stand ready if Hara'a turns to attack you."

The kings were in agreement to this. However, Arierona had something to add. "Our next action, then," said he, "must be to choose a new High King."

49. The House of Revaru

"We must have Ruapata here for the election," said Va'aru.

"A courier is already on the way," replied Hei'iro. "Hara'a must also be invited, for he is a king. We shall send one of the prisoners as messenger to him, promising his safety here." All seemed to agree with Hei'iro on this. None of them seemed to like it.

We rested now at the house of Revaru, which had, surprisingly, remained undamaged by war. Those who dwelt about that house seemed quite ready to welcome their young new king. Those who dwelt further away apparently were willing to accept him.

It was a pleasant land about that house, lush and fruitful, an orderly land of cultivated fields and villages. The house itself was like that of all the Mora and nearly as large as the now destroyed house of the High King. The kingdom of Revaru was a rich kingdom.

And a poor kingdom. I could see that in the people; here the commoners were descending into a sort of serfdom and the local nobles wielded much power over them. This kingdom, as much as any, showed one what lay behind the revolt. I could sympathize but I could never support the mad Hara'a or the traditionalist priests, who, after all, had twice attempted to assassinate me.

At last, Temani'itu had left the coast and the house of Va'aru, so he might preside over this election. Word was he traveled without great haste in our direction, by litter and accompanied by his sister, Lady Pua. Lord Hareata bore this news to us; he had hurried to the house of Revaru on hearing of our victory.

For victory it was, even if we had not defeated Hara'a. He had been driven back and that was enough, for now. With a new leader on the dais of the High King, the war could be carried to the rebel king.

I had time now, time for those things that might seem unimportant but truly are. It is not wars and politics that matter but those things for which the battles are fought, the deals are forged — peace and friendship and love, gardens and songs and even good beer. I had time to sit with Aranu and talk.

"The way is now open to the north," he told me. "We could travel there."

"Or Amirea could join us here," I responded. "The road seems safe and she is not that far along in her pregnancy."

He seemed uncertain about that idea, so I added, "If the right person suggested it, young Revaru would be glad to throw you a wedding feast here."

He mused on this. "My father wants what he calls a real wedding. You would officiate, would you not?" he asked, turning to me. Did the boy doubt it?

"I would be insulted if you did not allow me," I replied. "And if we are quick enough, we can do it while all the kings are still here. You will have even more than attended my wedding!"

The last of those kings soon arrived, first Ruapata with a small retinue. Most of his warriors remained in his kingdom; it would not do to leave it defenseless with Hara'a still a threat on his borders. Then Hara'a himself came.

HERO FROM THE SEA

None knew of it until he showed up before the house of Re-varu, dressed as an ordinary warrior, with a single companion. That did not say much for the security of the kingdom — what if he had been a spy, an assassin? Naturally, one could not mistake the king if one knew what to look for. His looks and his tattoos were both quite recognizable. He was given the hospitality of that house, a room for sleeping, meals when he wished, but none spoke to him.

He, however, sought me out. "I must apologize for the abuse of my hospitality by Tahu," said Hara'a. "It was right for you to slay the priest."

"It seemed the proper action at the time," was my reply. There was no discernible response to my attempt at humor.

"Yes, it was," he stated quite seriously. "It upset my plans for you, Hero. You were to give all the land its king and that king was to be me." What I saw in his dark eyes, some would name intensity. I knew it to be madness. "It will still be me, in time. This I believe."

"You will be no ones choice at this election, my Lord Hara'a."

"Oh, this I know. This crown, the false crown of the High Kings, will fall to earth, as foretold, and mine will rise. How could it not? The gods have told me so."

There was no arguing with that.

It was pleasant in the young king's house. He was a generous boy and fed his guests well. Beka's parrot had taken up residence here on his veranda and I suspected would remain after its owner had departed. And no sooner had Hara'a departed from me, Hareata took his place, coming to take a seat at my side.

"The king still hopes to woo you," he stated.

"That is a marriage that will not be," I asserted. "Speaking of marriages, what would you think of introducing our Revaru to Teme?"

"Teme? The young fellow would probably love the idea of taking the hero Poneiva's sister as his wife. Even more so if that hero becomes something greater." We both knew of what he spoke but no one there chose to say it aloud. There would come a proper time for that. "But that girl may be too ferocious for him. He will need someone more solid at his side to advise him."

"Well then, how about your niece? Far too young now, I know, but given some time, maybe."

"Yes, Tita might do well in that role. Smart and already knows her way around politics, having grown up in the High King's house."

"You have almost certainly already thought of that match, my Lord Hareata."

"Of course. But she truly is far too young for any serious consideration of such things. For that matter, so is Revaru. It wouldn't hurt for the two to meet someday." He regarded me and spoke frankly. "I'm more concerned about whom her mother might marry at this time."

"Not a pauper of a priest, I should hope. Guests arrive." A large party of warriors, attendants, and a pair of palanquins approached the house of Revaru.

HERO FROM THE SEA

"Ah, Temani'itu at last!"

50. A Choice

In a circle they sat, cross-legged on mats, feather crowns rising above their head. There was much red in those crowns, signifying their status as rulers. Temani'itu stood in their middle, slowly turning his massive body as he addressed them.

"We gather, kings of the Mora, to choose a new overlord. Who shall stand on the dais of the High King?"

Ruapata rose. "I name Poneiva." One by one, each of the other kings came to his feet. "Poneiva," stated Arierona, as did Avatu after him. "I too name Poneiva," said Hei'iro. Young Ruvaru stood and almost shouted, "Poneiva." Anana named him next, and then Va'aru. Mahutunoa rumbled, "I name the hero Poneiva," and turned his eyes to the one king who had not yet spoken.

"Who am I to go against all the kings of the Mora? Let Poneiva be High King." Hara'a's face remained passive, his voice calm, almost as if he dreamed before us. "The day comes there shall be no High King and the old ways will again be honored. The gods have seen that their people suffer!"

Poneiva rose and spoke. "Five days you have to return in safety to your own land, King Hara'a. Then your life is forfeit if I come upon you."

Within minutes, the king of the east and his single attendant left as they had come.

"I shall have to rebuild the house of the High King," Poneiva told the assembled rulers, "but there are more important tasks first."

"The defeat of Hara'a," asserted Ruapata.

"Clearing the rebels from my domain," Mahutunoa said.

"Both are important," agreed the new High King. "But foremost is reestablishing the watch on our coasts." There was a general murmur of agreement to that. "Then," he added, smiling broadly, "the wedding of my friend Aranu, son of Hei'iro. Warriors are escorting his bride south even now."

I wondered if Aranu had been aware of this. Or his father, for that matter. Certainly, no one had told me! Amirea on her way — could any of the others have been prevailed upon to accompany her? Oh, and I would have to prepare to act the role of priest again. Even if Teva was a symbol to me — I was about to say *only* a symbol, but there is nothing trivial about the symbolic — I would serve him to my best ability. In so doing, I served what Teva stood for, at least to me.

"For this I must remain," spoke Temani'itu. "Then shall I return to my home below the cliffs." He seemed to have finished, but after a brief rumination he continued. "And I would ask, High King, that your brother accompany me. I think he might someday serve you well there, even as I served my brother when he stood on the dais of the High King."

"If he wishes," replied Poneiva. "I fear he would miss his wife. As I miss mine." He nodded slowly, as if he had made a decision about something. "I must send for them both when I have a house!"

They would not be here for this wedding, however. It was two days later that the party from across the hills, from the trade town in Diwarna territory, made it to the house of Revaru. We had known they neared; there were scouts and messengers to keep us apprised of such things.

Exactly who made up the group of travelers was less certain. The only one we knew to expect was Amirea, Miss Amelia Nathan, Aranu's wife by Diwarna marriage and soon to be by Mora law, as well.

Not at all surprising was that her parents came with her, and the old steward Andrew Bailey, Andarua to the Mora. It was a bit of a trek, and none of them young, but how could they miss this? And who was that walking beside Amirea, the two chattering as if they were taking a casual stroll? Why, it was Demba and there were her brother and husband. The Diwarna woman had become very close to Amirea so perhaps I should have anticipated it.

Demba knew something now of the Mora from the trade town, so I doubted this place would intimidate her as had that village on her first visit. Oorto, of course, had seen things across the mountains that made the houses of the Mora kings seem insignificant.

"Diwarna are a curiosity on this side of the hills," remarked Hareata, who stood near me as Revaru gave an official welcome. "Many of our people have never seen them." This was true, as they rarely traveled beyond their own land. Even the half-breeds, save for the very few with Mora mothers, had no place here. Which led my thoughts to Ulani. Would he be coming?

"I do not know this either, Mika," Oorto told me when I had the chance to speak with him. "Nor whether he has been told that I am here." He turned his gaze from the gardens of Revaru to look fully at me. "I have spoken from afar with Rahaita, though briefly. We may attempt more now."

J.L. Nathan added, "He knows about the wedding, though. Ma'are made certain a messenger would stop at his teacher's house. What's his name?"

"Isa," Oorto said. "Taona Isa."

"Yes. Rather famous, isn't he?" The old man drew on his bamboo pipe, and our conversation lapsed for a minute or two.

"What of the rest of your party?" I asked Nathan. "I know that Dutch has found his place but what of the two seamen who accompanied you?"

"Diggs and Wise? I think that they will make that village their home. There are things to be done there and both have taken women. Here, they would be nothing. Across the hills, they're someone.

"But me, I don't know anything except sailing, so I'm going with Va'aru and Temani'itu when they leave here. Maybe I can teach them something, maybe not, but at least I will be by the ocean." It went without saying that his wife and faithful steward would accompany him.

"Perhaps," I said, "I shall travel with you on the way home to my wife." And that, I hoped, would be soon. After the wedding, there would be no need for my presence in the house of Revaru.

As far as I was concerned, I had done my duty as Hero from the Sea.

51. A Voice

"I shall admit, that if Hara'a remains quiet I would not be inclined to attack him," confided Poneiva.

I chose to speak what I knew to be truth. "He will not. He believes the gods have told him to follow the path to war." I wondered if Rahaita and Oorto had sought the man in visions. Of this, I would say nothing to the young High King; not now, anyway.

"The kings and I shall meet in council and make some decision." He shrugged. "Or Hara'a will make a decision for us. But we have more important things to discuss." Meaning, of course, our friend's wedding. "Beka and I will be taking charge of Aranu's cleansing rites tomorrow."

"Would that I could join in after what you three put me through!" My priestly dignity would not allow me that bit of fun.

"You officiated Heho's wedding, right? Good man, Heho. He should be on his way here." He smiled wistfully. "Possibly with messages from our wives."

"Let us hope there will be no need for messages soon."

Poneiva became rather sober. "Work has begun on building a new house of the High King, where E'eva can join me. I never foresaw such things in my life, Marareta." He sighed. "I could say it was you who brought them to me."

"You are not the only one whose path has taken unexpected turns, my friend. I only hope that mine leads at last to a peaceful life beside my own wife." Whether that be as a simple priest or as an adviser to her father.

"It is very strange to be part of a prophecy, Taona. Very strange."

"Maybe everyone is, Poneiva. They just don't know about it."

"Then they are fortunate."

"I think the Lady Pua wishes to speak to one or the other of us," I noted. She hesitated a short distance from where we sat on Revaru's front steps. That was a very un-kingly place for Poneiva to rest but he was allowed to do as he wished.

"She will have to take both," he replied and waved her to us. For the self-assured noblewoman to hold back so seemed unusual.

"My lords," she said, carefully taking a seat to the High King's left. "What is to become of me? I — I have served all my life but no longer know my place."

"Wouldn't your husbands like to see more of you, my lady?" I asked, and almost immediately regretted the attempt to lighten things.

But no harm done; indeed, she smiled at the remark. "Their status depended much on mine, Taona. Many opportunities existed for a brother-in-law of the High King." Pua spoke quite seriously now. "Temani'itu will probably wish to keep Naio with him, as in the past. It had been hoped that he would succeed him there with the fleet." Her eyes flickered briefly to the new High King's face. "But it would be right for Beka to now receive that honor."

"My brother knows something of the sea but is quite ignorant otherwise. He will need knowledgeable men beside him." Poneiva chuckled. "If I can even talk him into going." The man was entirely likely to choose his wife over holding a high position. Knowing that wife, however, I was certain Miruhata would send him off to sea. She had ambitions for Beka.

"My other spouse served among the house nobles of Maitoa. It is certain that he was slain when that house burned." Neither of us had known anything of this. From the look on Poneiva's face, I was sure someone would pay for not having informed him. He was fitting into the role of High King as if he had been born for it.

True, he had been born for it, in a sense. But certainly never expected to rule. "I mourn with you, Lady Pua," he spoke. "And know that I prize your words. You will always be welcome in the house of the High King."

She bowed her head graciously. "When it is built, my Lord Poneiva. Perhaps I shall spend some time with my sister-in-law at the house of Hareata." Now she looked at me in a way that made me just a tad uncomfortable. Still harboring thoughts of matching me with that widow? Or maybe with herself! Then she looked past me. "Is that my son coming? And Heho!"

I turned. Yes, Ulani and the courier approached the house, unescorted. They must have traveled so from the house of Isa. Two half-Mora they were, one with a Diwarna mother, the other a Kohari father, but now both accepted as part of this society. "Ho, Lady Pua," called Heho, "and Taona Marareta. Be this our new High King sitting on the steps like a boy from the country?" He grinned broadly at Poneiva, who could not help grinning back. He was, indeed, a boy from the country.

"I can leave this young fellow with you now," he continued. "He has worn my ears out with his poems and chatter."

HERO FROM THE SEA

Ulani stepped forward, not at all ill at ease. That was his training as a storyteller, no doubt; as Isa, he expected to be honored in any assembly, and he had grown greatly in confidence in this land. "My Lord Poneiva, I give my greetings to you. You too, Taona. I see you are no worse for having disappeared in the night." He turned to his adoptive mother. "Lady Pua, it is very good to see you again."

I think she might have preferred to be addressed as Mother, but she did not correct the lad, only rose and embraced him. She had lost another son, yes, and a husband, but she had Ulani.

"Oorto is about somewhere," I told him. "I think he would like to see you."

"I thought he might come." The young poet seemed a bit indifferent to the news. Had he hoped his lover — or was that former lover — would not travel here? "I shall go seek him."

"And I should recite all my many messages. For you, Taona, and Lord Poneiva. Then, I think, I shall never carry another man's words anywhere again."

We walked with Heho, the High King and I, as he spoke. There was little in his words that pertained to matters of state but much that pertained to our homes and our wives. At last, he said, "The Lady Rahaita wishes to join — so she described it — with the Diwarna shaman while you are all here. She thinks it would be best if you were present. They will seek Hara'a she says. I do not understand this but I know it is important."

I glanced at Poneiva. He would not really understand it very well either, though being around Pana'a and her prophecies all his

230

life would help. We should have Aranu there. He was much more familiar with their linking, having traveled with both Oorto and Rahaita across the mountains. There the two had discovered and developed their abilities under the guidance of the wizard Hurasu, the Lord of Visions.

All this I told Oorto, as soon as I found him. Or found him no longer distracted by Ulani. "It was good to see my beloved," he told me, attempting to keep the sadness from his voice, "but I think it unlikely we shall ever meet again. I shall return to the swamps of my people and he will become an honored story teller among his." There was nothing I could say about this so I did not try. "I shall attempt to speak afar with Rahaita tonight and perhaps we can find Hara'a, adrift somewhere, and hear his voice." He did not sound overly hopeful.

52. Journeys Begun

Poneiva was there, and his brother Beka, neither really knowing what was going on. Aranu came, and his father with him. That latter surprised me greatly. Aranu would begin his purification rituals in the morning and be married the day after.

Hito also accompanied them. He too had witnessed such beyond the high mountains. Ulani came not. "He is catching up with Lady Pua this evening," Oorto confided to me. "It is just as well. I would not have him remember me so." He had been only a naive boy when they had met; now he was a powerful sorcerer.

"It is always possible that others will intrude on our meeting," he continued. "That is ever a danger." Of this I was well aware, and feared for Rahaita's safety when she sought among the many worlds other than our own. He composed himself, sitting cross-legged on the floor, we six in a rough semicircle before him.

Silence. Then a faint smile on the Diwarna's dark face. "I'll tell him," he whispered. Was he speaking to my wife? Nothing for a while, nothing but a small movement of a hand, a shifting of weight, a change of expression. He stiffened, suddenly, then relaxed. I rather wished I had a watch so I might know how much time elapsed. No one counted the minutes in this land.

But it could have been no more than a quarter of an hour. Oorto's eyes flickered open and he stared at us a moment or two, uncomprehending, before breathing deeply and asking, "Is there any beer?"

Aranu laughed and handed him a bowl. "I knew you would need it, Master Oorto!" Hei'iro exhibited no understanding of what had just happened.

"He has traveled beyond this world, as do the seers on the Sacred Isle," Poneiva whispered to the king. "We'll give him a little time to gather himself." That was reasonably accurate so I felt no need to add further explanation.

"We met as we had planned," said the shaman, after a long drink. He addressed me and continued to do so. "It saves time to have a place chosen beforehand. Of ourselves and our homes we spoke for a few seconds. Rahaita sends you her love." He smiled gently. "Of course.

"Then we sought through the darkness for the one named Hara'a. Had we not know whom we sought we would never have found him. He is like a canoe adrift, lost, but not yet swept away. His ears are full of the words that pass through the void and he thinks them meant for him. But he recognized Rahaita when we touched him."

Oorto shuddered slightly. "I do not sense evil in Hara'a, not as we did in Teshum." That was the powerful wizard who had nearly destroyed my wife. "But he is obsessed with what he sees as his destiny. Also," he added, "he is obsessed with Rahaita. Maybe he thinks she is his destiny too."

That, I did not like at all. "Does he have any power?" I asked. "Is he a danger to either of you?"

"Definitely not, if we leave him be. If either engaged with him, he might be able to lash out, not knowing what he did."

"Then leave Lord Hara'a be," spoke Poneiva, "and allow my army to deal with him." We could all agree with that idea. "Now," he went on, "you had best get some rest, Aranu, and prepare yourself for tomorrow."

I, too, needed to prepare myself the next day, brushing up on the rituals, finding myself an appropriate costume — though I intended to wear my little feathered crown that Pua had made — making sure the time and place were as they should be. Revaru's garden was that place and sunset was the time. I argued for noon, as Hoka had insisted upon for my ceremony, but no one agreed.

It did give the groom more time to recover. The bride would have her own rituals, naturally, of which I was only vaguely aware. No swimming at the Pool of the Moon for Amirea, but there would surely be a local alternative to that ceremony. And, being decidedly pregnant, she hardly had a need to petition for fertility anyway.

Compared to the wedding of Poneiva and Beka to their brides, or my own to Rahaita, it was a rather small affair. No crowds of commoners filled Revaru's gardens through the daylight hours, nor were the noble feasters that evening particularly numerous. But they did include eight kings, not to mention the High King himself. Amirea and Aranu definitely had the bragging rights there.

Many of those kings would turn toward their own houses in the next day or two. The war was not over, no, but they could attend to other duties now and leave things, for a while, to their new

High King. Many men would be left behind for that High King to command.

I chose not to sit with those kings, arrayed to the right of the bride and groom, on that night. There had been enough feasts for me, enough high places. Oorto, Ulani, and I found a spot elsewhere in the royal gardens, and there celebrated less conspicuously with Pua and Heho. Other feasters joined us or left us as the evening progressed, warriors, minor noblemen. Demba — or Poa'ave, as all the Mora had taken to calling her — and Gordie ate with kings, at the bride's insistence.

In his way, Gordie was halfway to being a king in his own land. He had definitely made himself the most wealthy man on the north side of the hills in a rather short amount of time. I suspected that the Mora would find, soon enough, that they no longer controlled their little trade town.

That is a tale some other man may tell someday. My interests lay to the south and I hoped to be on the road soon. For now, though, I could enjoy this feast, smell the blooms in these gardens of Revaru, watch the pretty Mora girls pass, illuminated by the many torches (Rahaita wouldn't mind me noticing, would she?), look into the starry sky and know that those lights, once strange to me, were now my stars. This was now my place.

Hareata came and sat with us. It is notable that he gave me precedence in our little group, taking a place to my right. Perhaps it was only because of my role as officiating priest that night, perhaps it was because I was wed to the daughter of a king. Or maybe he saw me as the Hero from the Sea. He helped himself from the bowls scattered on the mat before us, then spoke. "I shall remain with Lord Poneiva and his brother while they put things to right in the lands of the High King," he told us. "The house must be rebuilt." He turned to Pua. "I trust you will reside in that house at times."

"Perhaps. For now, I think I will rest in yours for a while, Lord Hareata."

"You are always welcome there, my lady, as are all of you," he stated. But he glanced only briefly at the others. "You accompany Lord Temani'itu when he departs?"

"Lady Pua and I shall travel with him," I said, "as will Hei'iro and Va'aru and the newlyweds as well."

"And Neatanu," added Heho, "with his wife and Andarua." All the Nathans. J.L. had mentioned this plan.

"What of you, Heho?" asked Hareata. "Do you truly plan to leave us?"

"I do." He sounded very sure of it. "I shall accompany Demba and Gordie home. And once I am there with my wife, I think I shall not return to this land nor carry anyone's messages again."

"But I shall most certainly come and visit, Friend Heho," I said.

He laughed. "Perhaps, Taona, if your wife permits it. I do not know who else travels north with me." He peered toward Oorto and Ulani.

"I go home too," Oorto quietly said.

53. Separate Ways

Partings are painful. We all know this. Demba and Amirea embraced tearfully, pledging to visit each other. Whether either would be able to manage it, I could not say. Amirea and Aranu would be making their residence in the far south, in the house of Arierona. For now, though, they would journey to his father's home, continuing to Hei'iro's house once we reached Lake Aedina.

The parting of Oorto and Ulani could have been no less painful, if not as demonstrative. There were no illusions there of meeting again. Yet one never knows, does one?

Heho, too, embraced Ulani, before turning to his little group of travelers. Had he not watched the young storyteller grow up at the trade village? Then the four walked north, their figures slowly dwindling. They were without escort at Heho's request, though Poneiva had wished to assign a detail of warriors. Better they be just another group of travelers on the road, felt the courier.

Ulani sighed very deeply, exaggeratedly so, maybe. He was a professional storyteller, after all, and knew his way around dramatic gestures. They no doubt become second nature to one after a time. "It is better so, is it not?" he asked, apparently expecting no answer, for he turned and walked away from us.

"He intends to remain with Poneiva for now," Aranu said, low enough that only I heard him. "I think he will visit us again at the house of Arierona one day." More loudly, he told the others there, "Lord Temani'itu is ready to depart. Prepare to join him."

Within the hour, we were on the way toward Aedina and the house of Va'aru. In our midst, Lord Temani'itu rode in his sedan chair, but the kings Hei'iro and Va'aru walked as any others might. That was the way of the Mora.

With us also walked a sizable number of warriors, men who followed both kings. Many more remained behind for Poneiva to command. King Arierona chose to stay for a while longer, for his connections to the new High King were many, and with him, Aranu's second, Hito. No one believed the war or the rebellion to be over. We did not pass near the ruined house of the High King on this trip, but travled further to the west, crossing the Teiri into Va'aru's realm. Some of us swam that river, which was wide here though not deep. Va'aru himself plunged in to cross. Others were ferried on rafts, along with our weapons.

By this route it was not overly far to Aedina. "It's been a long time since I've seen that lake," commented James Nathan. "Not since we first arrived in this land. Now it looks like I'll be settling down by it."

"Right now?" I asked. "Or will you travel on to Hei'iro's house?"

"We go no further. The newlyweds don't need Judith and me tagging along." He gazed across the water at the house of Va'aru. "I switched my allegiance to our old friend here, but I expect to spend more time with Temmi." So he and Temani'itu were on nickname status?

"As long as Hueta doesn't have to live on the beach."

He nodded absently. "Andrew is getting too old for that sort of thing too. They'll want to enjoy Va'aru's hospitality."

"We all will as soon as we get across." We were nearing the water's edge and waiting canoes, the large ones that Temani'itu kept at Aedina among them. I turned to my left, looking to where Teoma broadened into the lake, longing to follow its course southward. Then I boarded a canoe and crossed with the rest.

Almost any reason is good enough for a feast in the house of Va'aru. So many distinguished guests guaranteed it. It was doubtful that I would sit down with many of these ever again, nor even lay eyes on them. I was prepared to take a low seat at the feast that night, in the great central room, but was directed to a place just to the right of Temani'itu. Only Hei'iro sat closer to out host.

Aranu, at my own right, whispered to me, "We are seen as pretty much equals, Taona, the husband of a king's daughter, the son of a king. But your priesthood and your status as prophesied hero give you the precedence this time." He chuckled. "And your advanced years."

"Be civil to your elders, boy," I warned him. "I'm a friend of the High King, you know."

"Very good with your fists, too, I know. You are the friend of many kings now, including my father." He passed a bowl of taro paste to me. I sniffed it and passed it on to my left. "He likes you."

"Which you should know is unusual," Temani'itu rumbled into my other ear, in an approximation of a whisper. The three of us could not help taking a quick look at Hei'iro, who seemed to be in serious conversation with Va'aru. Va'aru, I think, would rather have been paying attention to his meal.

"Will you travel with me tomorrow?" continued Temani'itu. "Neatanu and I go to the cliffs."

"And Amirea and I head for my father's house," said Aranu. "We hope to see you by A'auwa before too long."

"I do long for A'auwa and my wife," I replied. "But I need not start my journey up Teoma right away. I shall accompany you, Lord Temani'itu."

"Waiting for my sister to conclude her business here, eh?" I should have expected the admiral to know that I had agreed to escort her to the house of Hareata.

"That is so," I acknowledged. "The Lady Pua must not be hurried."

54. Safe Harbor

"Ah! The logs for my new canoes are here." Temani'itu gazed out over the wide cerulean bay below the Great Falls. I could see two very large tree trunks, pulled partway onto the beach. Were they the ones the Kohari had been cutting when I passed down the Gurang?

When we had all been lowered down the cliffs, I found this to be so. Poyo and the men I had met on the river were among the crowd gathered around those huge logs. Several other tree trunks of varied size were also beached there, near the outlet of the lagoon. Mora were examining them, checking grain and knots, arguing about how best to approach the carving of each, whether they were better suited to the construction of canoes or huts.

Temani'itu stood a while and looked at them. "I had hoped for a larger one," he said at last. "I have wished to create the greatest of canoes while I still could."

"It was difficult enough to get these ones here, Master," said one of the Kohari. "The weather made us fear for our lives. Almost did we cut all our hard won timber loose!"

"That little bit of a blow?" chided a Mora sailor. "Wait for Wanga to throw a real storm at us some day!"

"Wanga? It was the great serpent Bagap, coiling and uncoiling at the bottom of the sea." The Kohari who said this did not sound at all serious about it. As I had noted before, the Kohari traders were seemingly not very religious.

"Maybe Wanga nipped him," suggested a Mora, to outright laughs all around.

"I know a way to make a larger vessel, Lord Temani'itu," I said in a low voice.

"What, put it together from pieces of wood, like the Kohari? You were going to show us that craft, weren't you Neatanu?" He turned to J.L Nathan.

"Yes, but with honest joints and pegs, not sewn together like their boats."

"You have seen double canoes in your voyages, have you not?" I asked Nathan.

"That I have, that I have." He nodded his head thoughtfully. "That is not at all a bad idea, my boy." I left him to explain the concept and walked down to the water's edge. Small waves rolled in, washing about my ankles. Far off to the northwest lay the islands we had first encountered in this world. It seemed unlikely now that I would ever glimpse them again, though at the time I and my comrades had considered making one of them our home. How different things might have been had we not sailed on, seeking our missing shipmates.

I turned and looked toward the high cliffs, the great waterfalls where Teoma fell to the sea. There was where my destiny had led me, even as prophesied by the priestesses of this land. And what now awaited me? Had I accomplished all that was foretold? Could I now fade into the legends of these people, the Hero of a long past world?

Suddenly I longed very much to be with Rahaita.

That night I drank palm wine again with the Kohari traders, listened to the playing of the sef, but my heart was not there. "I must return to my home, Poyo," I told my host. "There is nothing for me by the ocean."

"Every sailor seeks his home port, one day," he agreed, and then laughed. "There are many songs about it," he said, and launched into one. Yes, there were many songs in my world, too. Men everywhere sought a safe harbor.

The next morning I made my goodbyes and climbed a lengthy rope to the top of the cliffs. Before the end of the day, I had crossed the long, swaying suspension bridge across the Teoma, climbed the stairways by the waterfalls, and stood before the house of Va'aru.

There seemed a great turmoil there, many men coming and going. "There was fighting to the north," I was told when I waylaid one of them. "It is rumored that the king's cousin was slain."

"Hareata?" He nodded and hurried away on whatever business he had. Perhaps I should seek out Pua.

That did not prove difficult, for she sat alone on Va'aru's west porch, above his gardens. I sat wordlessly by the tall noblewoman's side. "We do not know if Hareata lives or was slain," she said, without preliminaries. "A rebel force attacked the patrol he accompanied."

"Hara'a has returned?"

She shook her head. "No, it was one of the bands of commoners who have risen against us." Us — was I part of this 'us?' "I have heard nothing of Hara'a. I have heard little of anything." There was frustration in her voice. Lady Pua did not like being shut out of what was going on.

"What course do you wish to follow, my lady?" I asked.

"That which we already intended — it would be all the more important now to be at Hareata's house. Will you go with me in the morning?"

The garden was falling into the shadows of dusk. "I will."

"I thank you." Pua turned to me, her speech measured, but her face betraying her concern. "If Hareata has fallen, Panoha needs a protector more than ever. And now Mehetu, as well."

I owed many debts to Lord Hareata. If this was how I might repay them, by providing for his sister and his widow, then I would do it. "Very well," I said. "If Hareata is dead I shall take Panoha as my wife. If she wishes it." Rahaita would understand; indeed, she would probably have urged it on me.

"The house of Hareata would become the house of Marareta, as long as you lived. But we need not speak of such things now. The Lord Hareata may live." The lady managed the ghost of a smile. "Offer a prayer for him, Taona, when you have the time."

She sighed. "Once again, I will not have the time to see Naio. Was he with Lord Temani'itu?"

Her remaining husband. "I do not know, my lady. If he was there, he never was presented to me."

"Hmm, probably at sea again, then. Naio loves being on the water more than being with me." I wondered if Naio or the slain husband — whose name I had never heard mentioned — had been the father of the High King Ve'eta. It didn't matter, did it?

"His loss then, my lady," I responded. "I should pay my respects to Va'aru, and find sleep if we are to get an early start." I rose and left her, still seated, watching servants light torches in the king's gardens.

In the dark before sunrise, we two, and only we two, paddled south out of Lake Aedina and up the broad Teoma.

55. Prayers

"Is this your new attendant?" asked Tita, all pretend innocence.

"Your poor aunt needed a position," Pua told the girl. "My new master only beats me now and then."

Tita turned to me. "You mustn't spoil your servants, my Lord Marareta." Unable to contain herself longer, she giggled. The girl was less like her aunt than I had first thought, and more like her father, more open. Surely some part of this self-possessed young lady grieved for that father, the late High King, though it had been more than a year since his passing.

"I shall try my best, Tita. And please do not call me lord."

She glanced at her aunt, perhaps uncertain whether she had made some faux pas. She was just a little girl, after all. "Taona would be the proper title, my dear," she was told.

How Tita had happened to be at the river when we arrived, I do not know. Perhaps she went there frequently; there was certainly little of interest for her in the house of Hareata, nor anyone to play with. On the banks of Teoma, she could be just another child.

We three followed the path to that house. "You married what's-her-name after leaving here, didn't you?" asked the girl.

"Rahaita. Yes, I did."

"Rahaita," she repeated. "She's a king's daughter so you *are* a lord! Even if you don't want to be."

"I can not argue that point, my lady, but I still don't like being addressed so."

She nodded her head. "Very well. So don't call me lady, either."
Tita led us up the steps and into the house of her uncle.

"Have you any news?" were the first words from Lady Mehetu.

"None," said Pua, moving forward to embrace the wife of
Hareata. "We shall await word with you." She glanced toward me.
"I know not how long the Taona can tarry here."

"You are welcome in our house as long as you wish to remain,
Taona Marareta," said Mehetu. "It is understood that you would
wish to continue your journey home."

"I thank you for your hospitality, my lady," I replied, as formally as she had offered her invitation. I made no commitment one
way or another as to the length of my visit. That might depend on
what news came in the next day or two.

Mehetu was just the sort of person who would use formality
and ceremony to keep order in her life, quite unlike Pua. The two
must be of about the same age, I thought, and though it would be
impolite to ask, I would guess that age to be not so much greater
than my own.

Indeed, less than the difference between Rahaita and myself.
How old was I now, anyway? I had quite lost track of things like
that. Not too old — that is all that matters, isn't it?

Panoha joined us after a time. This, naturally, reminded me of
the promise I had made to Pua. I would say nothing of that unless
it became necessary. And surely the High King's widow had suit-
ors by now — she might not be interested in me at all.

But I saw none. It was I and the three women at our evening
meal, Tita being considered still too young to sit with adults. I

wondered when that changed. Teme, at fourteen, had a place at the feasts of Arierona. We spoke only of little things at that meal.

Undoubtedly, Hareata was on the mind of each of us. He was the first Mora I ever met, the man who had come north to the swamps of the Gurang to seek out the strangers from the sea, our band of castaways. That he had wished to use us was never in question, but we were not misused. Hareata had been my friend.

As I fell asleep that night, in a small room near the rear of the house of Hareata, I did offer that prayer Pua had requested. To whom did I address it? To any god and all, to the God of the world to which I was born, to Teva whom I had adopted here.

And as I slept, I dreamed, dreamed as I had once at the Place of the Crocodile. Then my dreams had been the sending of a powerful sorcerer. Were these, or were they born only of my own concerns and fears? I had seen too much in this world to have ready answers, pat solutions. Maybe even Teva was real and more than an idea. My dreams all told me one thing — to go home.

This I announced in the morning, nor did I hesitate to say that dreams had told me to go. This no longer seemed strange to me. As I prepared, though, a messenger arrived, sent from Poneiva.

He was directed to seek out not only the women of the house of Hareata but also me, and so was happy to find us all together and know he would need not pursue me up the river. "Lord Hareata lies wounded," he told us. "It is not known whether he will live." He looked at the wife and sister of the fallen warrior. "So is my message worded. I am sorry that this is so, my ladies. The lord was struck in the head by a slung stone and remains as one asleep."

A coma. There would be no treatment for that here, no way to feed the man while he lay unconscious. "It is thought the attack might have been a feint while Hara'a readied to strike elsewhere, perhaps toward Ruapata's realm before he returns. There are only rumors of this."

But it made sense. "Then I have all the more reason to return quickly to my home," I stated. "Do you carry this message to others?" I asked the courier.

"No, only here. Others carry words to Va'aru, or west to Hei'iro."

"Then when you return to the High King, tell him I on my way to the house of Arierona." I spoke to the women. "Have you any messages to send back?"

They looked to each other before Mehetu answered, "None. There is nothing to be said."

"Nothing but prayers," said Panoha.

56. Fate

Alone, I paddled south against the current of the Teoma. It's flow was powerful, the result of recent storms that had swept in from the ocean to dissipate in rain upon the far mountains. I chafed at the slowness of my progress, thinking I might do as well to take to the road.

One man and one paddle. It was an uneven fight but fight I did, past the mouth of the Teiri, past the river that led to the house of Isa, flowing down through fragrant groves. I almost did not recognize the first fall when I reached it, for it more resembled rapids.

Rapids I could not pass, that was certain. I left my canoe there and strode on, a staff in my hand, a pack basket on my back. I owned nothing more in this world than what I carried. That did not matter; all I wanted or needed waited ahead.

The falls known as Pana'a could be heard roaring as I passed by. The Pool of the Moon might not be a good spot to bathe right now, with that torrent pouring into it. Then I beheld A'auwa, swollen but yet within its shores. This, I had been told, was common enough in seasons of rain.

Darkness approached, and a waxing crescent stood in the sky. Lightning flickered in the distant northwest. There were lights at the house of Arierona, torches before its entry, lamps within. The scent of the palm oil burning in those lamps of hollowed stone would fill the house.

I could see lights flickering, too, on the Sacred Isle. How did those priestesses entertain themselves on such nights? No ascetics were they, despite the prohibition against men on their island. Did they sing or play at games? Did they gossip of lovers they had visited? That island was high, a mass of rock in A'auwa, so flood waters would be of no concern there.

Then Rahaita was in my arms. "You took long enough," she whispered in my ear.

"Blame the floods of Teoma," I told her. "You knew I was coming?"

"You were spied on the road and a servant ran to tell me." We entered the wide front portal. "Oorto told me that he tried to send you messages wrapped in dream, to hurry you along."

"Ah! So that explains them. Hurasu sent such dreams once."

"I have avoided reaching toward my teacher. Oorto, I think, has spoken with him from afar." That should concern neither of us.

"Has any news of Hareata reached here?" I asked.

Rahaita stopped walking and turned to me. "Lord Hareata sits with the gods. The message arrived two days ago." Tenderly, sadly, she spoke. "I know he was a great friend of yours, Marareta."

"He was. I owed him much." I would have to speak to her of my promise. This was not the time for that, nor to mourn for Hareata. We continued toward our rooms.

"Hepetea is with the baby," she informed me, just outside the entry. "Miruhata and E'eva have left to be with their husbands. Poneiva, the High King! It is hard to believe."

"It is. I am not sure he believes it himself."

HERO FROM THE SEA

"It was fate," asserted Hepetea, who had heard the end of our conversation. "Maratoa sleeps in the Lady Rahaita's room. Your room," she corrected herself. "Should I bring him to you, Taona?"

"Time enough for that, Mistress Hepetea. Is your husband about?" A quick glance around the room revealed two rolled-up mats. Were she and Rika sleeping here?

"I sent him for food. We doubted you would want to go any further than these chambers tonight." Without further comment, she began laying out mats for serving and seating. Two distinct settings, I noted, so that the commoners could share our meal without actually sitting with us. Not a one of us would have minded that but Mora did these things without thinking about it, most of the time.

Rika brought not only food but a servant carrying more food. Good man, Rika. Fruit and freshly roast pork and the ubiquitous taro concoctions came out of their baskets. Beer? I looked for the typical wooden bowl. Oh, an actual earthenware crock! I had no doubt that it had come from the north, from the trade village, but certainly hadn't expected anything of the sort to show up here yet.

"Amlee and Tala made sure this came to us, " said Rahaita, as she poured a bowl of millet beer for me. "People come by at all hours just to admire it." It was truly a bit crude and the designs painted on it were cruder, but it was a beginning. There would be more pottery coming south.

So we ate and I said little. I was too busy looking at my wife. Yet my thoughts went also to Hareata and all the rest that had befallen. Had these things simply happened? Was there no reason for any of them?

"You believe in fate, Hepetea?" I asked, remembering her earlier remark.

She looked up from the yam she was peeling. "Were there not prophecies, Taona?"

"Those do not make the future," Rahaita said. "They only tell us of it."

Hepetea took a moment to digest this and then nodded her head. "I suppose that is so, my lady. But how could the future be seen were it not already fated to be?" She smiled at her own logic. "It was fated that the Hero from the Sea would come."

"I wonder if I did not bring as much grief as good. If I am your Hero."

She shrugged. "Whether you are he, Taona, or Lord Bafa or even Beka, there was a Hero and now Poneiva rules us all. That can not be denied!"

"No, it can not," agreed Rahaita, with a smile.

"Your fate has touched all of us. Did you not take Rika away and bring him back when I thought him surely dead? Returned him a better man than he was, too!"

"That you did," agreed her husband. "You showed me wonders. It changes a man." Rika was right about that. None of us had come home the same.

"It was meant to be. And you brought back this willful girl, grown into the woman she was meant to be. Meant for *you*, Taona." I might have told her Rahaita could still be quite willful.

"So you are the woman of wisdom and experience now?" asked Rahaita, her laugh gently mocking. "You are no more than two years older than I, Hepetea."

"Therefor, two years wiser! And wise enough to hold my tongue now." Her giggle did not at all suggest wisdom.

Whether fate or luck or random happenstance had brought me home, I knew I *was* home, at last. Home with my wife, with my son. Home by the broad A'auwa, the lake I had come to love. In the dark, as I held Rahaita, I spoke of my memories of Hareata, and of my sorrow and my promise.

"That would be a good thing, Beloved. You know I do not object to Panoha."

"And you know I do not love her as I do you."

"Of course not," she sleepily replied. "You say some very foolish things, Marareta."

57. Refuge

Refugees were at the thresholds of Arierona's house, driven before the army of Hara'a. Through the lands of Ruapata had he swept, scattering the men that king had left behind. But he did not linger there, instead driving on toward A'auwa.

There was no hope that Arierona could return home with his troops before the rebels reached us. But Ponu was not helpless. He still had many men, and more were coming in from the houses of the far-flung vassals. Amapa, father of Poneiva and Beka, was there with a troop; some I noted were Kohari, freedmen who now served him or slaves who were promised their freedom.

And I must fight again, it seemed. "I shall stand with you, Taona," stated Rika. I would rather he remained and guarded my family, but I did not say so. Not yet. I was weary, I admit. I needed time to think on things. In the early morning, I launched a canoe onto A'auwa, skirting the low, rocky cliffs about the Sacred Isle, and crossed to where lay the shrine of Teva.

Who better than old Hoka to speak with? At the least, he might share some of his homemade wine with me. But another waited by the statue of Teva.

"Hoka is busy eating his breakfast and complaining to his wives," spoke Pana'a, turning to greet me. "You seem troubled. Will you sit with me?"

"I have my own complaints, I fear," I told her, as we settled onto a log placed there as a seat. It was old and mossy and would soon need replaced. "I have helped those around me find their places, but can not seem to find where I belong. I thought perhaps becoming a simple priest might bring me peace. That does not seem the way either." I shrugged. "Even Hoka said it was not my place."

"But you do have Rahaita." Her smile was bittersweet. "And our son."

"That is what keeps me here. I am no priest, nor a fighting man, nor a noble. What am I?"

"Some of each, maybe." A moment's hesitation. "Lord Poneiva would like to name you High Priest." She laughed at my astonishment. "Yes, there are those who bring such tales to me. It would be poor politics and you would not want the position, I am sure."

"One might be tempted by such power, and the good that could be done." For a moment, perhaps I *was* tempted but Michael Malvern was certainly no 'white savior' as in adventure novels, come to bring enlightenment to the savages. I continued. "I suspect it would be hard to really change much of anything." Amlee and Tala's pottery might change this land more quickly than any High Priest could.

"This is true. Even all that you have already done has truly changed little in our homeland."

"What then is my place?"

Her thick dark eyebrows knit in thought. Pana'a's appearance was like that of Rahaita in many ways, but bolder in her features, her nose more prominent. "That is something you have sought all your life, is it not, Marareta?" She sighed deeply. "Unlike I, who was always destined to abide on the Sacred Isle and prophecy to the Mora nation.

"Sometimes I wish I might go and seek as well. I envy you the chance to do so." Apparently wishing to speak no more of this, she changed the subject.

"You can send Rahaita to us on the island if you fear for her safety."

"But what of my son? She would not leave him." All males were prohibited on the the Sacred Island, no matter what their age.

"He might be more safe with Hepetea and Rika. Send them somewhere. The house of Amapa, perhaps."

That made much sense. But — "Why not Rahaita, as well?"

She spoke now with great seriousness, weighing each word. "Hara'a can feel her presence. I think he will follow here wherever she is. On the island, we might be able to hide her. It is a place of power and all we who live there have gifts." She then seemed to consciously attempt to lighten her tone. "Let us hope it is unnecessary, and his army is defeated."

There was something there. Had Pana'a seen some future of which she would not, could not, tell me? I knew there was no sense in pressing her. She rose. "I return to my island, Marareta. Go drink wine with Hoka but do not pester him with questions."

I took that as good advice and did as she said. It was late when I returned, paddling to the shore as the sun sank behind the house of Arierona. My intention was to go straight to my wife, but Ponu waylaid me. "I wish you to remain and guard the house of my uncle," said the nobleman, "while I march to meet Hara'a's army."

I was to be in charge here? That's what comes of marrying a king's daughter. Even as Pana'a, I had not real choice. But later — yes, when this war was over, we would be free of such restraints.

Following my conference with Arierona's most likely heir, I hurried to my rooms and told Rahaita of her aunt's advice. "I do not like this, Marareta," she told me. "But I know it is wise."

"You could travel north and be beyond Hara'a's pursuit," I said.

"Leave you and our child behind? No, my husband. And what if he did follow and overtook me?" She thought for a moment. "There will need to be a wet-nurse. Miri. I think her husband could accompany them. He is a gardener, you know." I did not. I'd been away. "And she has a child — I'd better go talk to Hepetea in- stead of you, standing there like a lump."

The whole group was on the road by mid-morning the next day. I assigned a couple warriors to go with them. I could do that, though I did not like to use the authority that went with my posi- tion as son-in-law of the king. Strictly speaking, I outranked Ponu in this house, but we both knew who was in charge.

And in another day, that would be me. Ponu readied his troops, gave last minute instructions to those who remained, those whom I nominally would command. Those officers were more capable than I but inevitably I would be called upon to coordinate them, to make final decisions. If no fighting reached us, it did not matter.

None the less, I made sure of my weapons, found a new spear, rubbed oil into my weathered wooden club. I looked at the carv- ings upon it as I worked, ornate scrolls and symbols. That one was for the family of Arierona, wasn't it? It was he who had gifted me this club, and I had never quite understood why. Maybe I just made a good impression on our first meeting.

Ha, little did he know I would be wedding his daughter!

Then I put that daughter on a canoe and sent her to her aunt.

58. *Rain*

"I am ready to defend the house, Taona!"

Before I turned, I knew who spoke. "Teme?"

I had watched Rahaita paddle away, into the distances of a rain-misted lake. In the complex Mora tongue, there would undoubtedly be a precise word for such a view, but I did not know it. Ponu with his army already marched south along A'auwa. Now that they were on the move — he had chafed at every delay and had wished to depart a day earlier — they would move swiftly to engage the rebel army. That, apparently, was advancing slowly but steadily.

But here was the sister of the High King, the daughter of Amapa, standing with a bow and quiver of arrows and a very determined expression. "How did you get here, girl?"

"I walked," came her answer. I suspected I would get none better from her. Sneaked away from her parent's house, perhaps, or they might think her safely with some other family. Even I knew how devious girls that age could be. Sometimes as devious as adults.

And there was nothing to be done about it. "Come and eat with me," I said. "We'll discuss your duties."

"Was that Rahaita?" she asked me as we walked toward the house.

"Yes. She'll be safer on the Sacred Isle, I think."

Teme accepted this without comment. "I'll be your only archer," she said. "All the rest are with Lord Bafa." She sounded as though she wished she were too.

"You could keep walking north and perhaps run into him," I told her. She wrinkled her nose at my attempted humor. "You will have to go visit your brother in his new house soon," I went on. Maybe she would meet young King Revaru there.

"When we have defeated his enemies," she stated. Hareata had been right; the girl was ferocious. I turned and surveyed the area before the king's house, once we had climbed the front steps.

"This is the place for you," I said. "You can keep a watch and release your arrows from here. And," I emphasized, "if danger draws near you, you are under orders to run as fast as you can the other direction!"

"I will, Taona. I know I can not fight a warrior." She grinned most wickedly. "Yet."

"I much doubt we will see danger here." We proceeded along the covered way and around the corner, to the eating porch. There was always something available here, a continuous buffet, even in the middle of the night.

"I hear you are taking a second wife, Taona," the girl commented, after stuffing herself for a while on melon and cold fowl.

"Perhaps." I saw no reason to explain.

She knew, anyway. "I will miss Lord Hareata," said Teme. "I hope the rebels do come here so I can slay many of them!" Perhaps, in my heart, I did as well.

As messengers sped back and forth, we found this might happen. Reports came that the first meeting of the two armies had been inconclusive, but that Ponu had fallen back to regroup. They also told us that a number of Ruapata's men had found their way to him. It would be many days before any more aid could come, from the north.

But while Ponu had engaged the main host further to the south, a smaller force had swung around them and now appeared at the head of A'auwa, only hours away from the house of Arierona. "It looks to be fewer than five hundreds," a courier told me and my captains. "It also seems that Hara'a himself leads them."

Five hundred men. Ponu had left me two troops of an hundred, but there were also many men about, both noble and commoner, who might be expected to stand with us. But should we fight, out-numbered, or withdraw and avoid battle? For me, there was no question of leaving while Rahaita was here.

"I would stand and fight," I told the two commanders. They were in thorough agreement.

"Let me take my men around so we might attack his flank," said the one.

The other approved. "And I will come at the front."

"While I organize those who remain here," I stated. "If you do not stop Hara'a, you can at least delay him." They would be buy-ing me time — we all recognized this. I must oversee both a de-fense and an evacuation.

Many of those who could not fight had already been sent away, before even Ponu had left. The rest must go now, the young, the old, most of the women — few Mora women trained with weapons but there were always exceptions. It was still raining, though not heavily. That should slow down the advance of the en-emy, giving us more time.

Time which ran out. First came our own men, falling back before the advance of the enemy. "We killed many, my lord," one warrior, weary yet still willing, told me. "But we could not stop them. We will stand with you again before the house of our king." I saw no sign of their officers; those must have fallen.

"Fetua," I called, recognizing one of the seconds among those who had retreated, "you must take charge here. Draw as many men together as you can but if you must abandon the house, do so. Your lives are more valuable to Arierona! I will take some men to the lakeside." I gathered some twenty or so warriors and led them to A'auwa.

To guard the road was my intention, and to guard my wife. I could not let Hara'a's men advance further north along the lake. It was assumed that they would strike first at our main force, drawn up between them and the house of Arierona. The match would not be too uneven; it might be possible to stop them.

I heard distant voices. "Those are taunts, Taona," said a man standing beside me. "They are not fighting yet." Why not?

The answer became evident when we spied a small group rushing up the pathway toward us. While the main force kept our men occupied, this troop had slipped by along the shore of A'auwa. Their number seemed roughly equal to our own. Did they intend to attack the house? There — Hara'a stood among his warriors. It might be Rahaita he sought.

An arrow whistled through the air, but fell short of the enemy. Too far away, Teme. I hoped she would have the sense to remain too far away. Then our two forces fell upon each other, and there would have been no target for the young archer.

That these were the king's best men, I have no doubt, his personal guard. We were outmatched. Hara'a himself was impressive in his skills, as fine a warrior as any, laying about himself with one of the heavy Mora spears, using the shaft more than the point. "Take the man from the sea!" he ordered his men. "Do not slay him."

Several of my followers lay dead or wounded already. It would do no good to continue this. "Fall back," I called. "Reform at the house!" We attempted to disengage, to back away. I am proud to say that not one turned and ran. Then I was again amid the press. Arms grasped at me, pinning me. My club was wrested from my hand.

"We have him, Lord!" someone called.

"Let the others go," came the king's response. Battle ceased, the two groups backing away from each other, glaring fiercely at their enemies.

"Go!" I yelled at my own troop. "Leave me!" There was hesitation on many faces but they obeyed.

"That is good, Hero," said Hara'a in his customary detached manner. It seemed almost as if he were not here at all, as if he were watching some amusement from a distance. "A leader should care about his men."

"Then he would not use them to attack another without need," I spat out. If two very large Mora men had not held me, I would have been at his throat.

He evinced no response to this, but continued his monologue. "I have come for Rahaita. It has been revealed that we are to be together. The gods have told me!"

"Rahaita is my wife. She seeks no other spouse."

He nodded absently. "Yes, yes. You must divorce. Rahaita can be mine only."

"That will not be." I spoke this truth quite emphatically.

"Then, Hero," the king told me, "you must die."

59. The Gods

Hara'a turned and looked toward the isle of the priestesses. "I know she is out there. It is a place of the gods, a place of power, but she shines more brightly than all the rest." The king walked down to the water's edge. "Come to me or I shall slay your husband!" he called.

I looked about me as Hara'a stood staring out onto the lake, waiting patiently, for three or four minutes. He had lost several men in our fight, more than I might first have guessed. Still, a dozen sound warriors were left him. One pointed into the lake. "My lord!"

"She comes," said Hara'a. A canoe was slowly making its way toward us. No, Rahaita, you should not. Paddle to the other shore of A'auwa, not to this madman!

Without any show of hurry, Rahaita pulled her canoe onto the shore and walked toward us. "What would you have of me, Lord Hara'a?" she asked. Rahaita could not have heard him from the isle but must have sensed his presence.

"I would have you, Lady Rahaita. I have known you were destined as my wife since I was a child, dreaming by the Blood Stone. I have felt your presence day and night.

"I took no other wife. The gods promised me you!" He rushed on. "We shall be as no others before us. We shall be gods too."

There he stood, that great, handsome, mad king, ensorcelled by his own powers, powers he might have understood if someone had shown him the way. This was the legacy of Hurasu in this world, the gift and the curse that he had passed to his descendants.

"I have a husband, my lord. I rather like him."

"The gods give and they take —" he began.

"The gods laugh at you! Don't you hear them?" Her voice came forceful, compelling.

His eyes opened wide. "I do! I do!" he whispered. "Why do they laugh?"

She was attempting to use her abilities, to speak with the Hara'a who wandered, the part of him lost among the infinite other worlds. Here, near the Sacred Island, his mind must be even more distracted by their relentless, chaotic presence.

"They laugh at you for thinking yourself their equal!"

He pulled himself together. "No. This is not what they have told me. You will come with me as my bride or I shall slay the Hero." It would seem Hara'a had practice controlling the voices in his head.

So she attacked directly. How often had Hurasu warned against such things? Even he, the greatest sorcerer of this world, the father of all sorcerers, feared to so act. Would that Rahaita had remembered his teaching. Would that she had not been risked her very soul so, risked it for me.

The two stood, facing each other, lost to the rest of us. I could hear fear and apprehension in the mumbling of my captors. Of a sudden, both fell back, gasping. "No!" cried Hara'a. "I will not go!" He snatched up his spear, wild-eyed, and threw it with all his force. Rahaita fell, transfixed.

HERO FROM THE SEA

The king panted, searching all around him but his eyes unseeing. "She would have locked me in the darkness forever!" Then his gaze focused and he saw Rahaita lying before him. "Aiee! What have I done? You were to be mine. It was promised! It was promised —" His voice trailed off.

Struggle though I might, I could not break free of those who held me. I could only look upon what had happened and scream to the heavens for the life of Hara'a.

I suppose he had thought only of his own plans, his obsession, but Hara'a had made a mistake in allowing my men to retreat. No sooner had they reported to Fetua than he sent a half hundred to my rescue. The two armies had still stood confronting each other across a field of freshly sprouted millet, neither attacking. Ours, because their task was to defend, Hara'a's because they had been ordered to await his return, if possible.

Now those men appeared, ready to engage Hara'a's warriors. These turned, prepared to defend their king to the death, though greatly outnumbered. I was released. I was free. I looked to where stood my wife's murderer.

Hara'a would be mine. My club dangled still at my right wrist, tethered there. I took it into my hand and rushed upon him. The shaft of his spear took me on the side of my head, sending me reeling.

Fool! I was no match for this warrior, despite my training, despite my background. I knew this. I could not defeat him anymore than I would be able to stand in the ring against Jack Johnson. But I did not fear him. I was beyond that point.

I would fight until one of us lay dead — this I swore to myself Always his spear was at the ready, to block, to thrust, to swing about and catch me with its shaft. Once, I landed to his ribs and he stepped back with a grunt. It was not enough. Again, his spear glanced off my head and then between my legs, sending me tumbling to the ground.

Hara'a loomed above me, a dark figure against a dark and stormy sky, ready for a final thrust of his spear. Suddenly, he toppled back.

An arrow jutted from his chest.

60. A'auwa by Moonlight

Teme stood at my side, her face streaked with tears. She had slain a man; for any fifteen year old, that in itself might be overwhelming, but much more had befallen this day. I pulled her to me, holding her as tightly as she held me.

"Rahaita?" she sobbed at last.

"She is —" It felt hollow to say that she sat with the gods. I did not know where Rahaita went. "She is gone."

Hara'a's guard had dispersed quickly when he fell, leaderless and outnumbered, running back to their main force. The report soon followed that the entire army he had brought so close to the house of Arierona had turned and retreated southward. Fetua allowed them.

My wife's form was wrapped in bark cloth and solemnly borne to her father's house. "Will you go with her, Teme?" I asked. "I do not think I can. Not right now."

"Yes, Taona. I will not leave the Lady Rahaita." She started to go and then turned back to me, stating vehemently, "I am glad I killed Hara'a."

"So am I, Teme. So am I." She followed the procession up the slope. I heard low, sad singing somewhere. I wished that I too could cry but there seemed no tears in me. There seemed nothing in me.

The girl had saved my life. Did I care? Had I gone through all these things, shipwrecks and wars, long and perilous journeys, only to come to this? It was for Rahaita I had risked my life. I was the Hero from the Sea for her sake.

When I had at last found that for which I had always sought, it was taken from me. Long, I sat and gazed out over the lake, and none dared intrude upon me. In the evening, the skies cleared and the moon stood near full above A'auwa.

There came a canoe. It was a long canoe bearing the priestesses of the isle, all but one of the six who dwelt there. One must always remain, I remembered. Silently, they disembarked, wordlessly they went their way toward the house of Arierona. Yet each stopped and bowed her head to me before proceeding.

The last came and sat beside me. Pana'a said nothing but only watched with me, watched the shimmering silver water, A'auwa by moonlight.

"Again I ask my place," I said after a while. "I am too weary to search further."

"Then this is the place to stop."

I pondered that a minute or so as we both sat, unspeaking. "Here, where all I had found was taken from me?" I asked at last. "Here where I once thought I might be happy?"

"Here where you are," the Priestess of the Moon replied. "You were as one lost when you came to this land, a man who knew not who he was. Here you have found yourself, found yourself in those who believed in you, those who became your friends, in she who loved you." She grew silent. Pana'a loved me too, did she not?

"Was it worth it?" I murmured.

"Do not count this as being without value. It was Rahaita's gift to you."

271

It was. She had given me myself. I felt tears at last. I could permit them now. A great sob escaped me and I wept, wept as I had never before and knew I never would again. The priestess waited patiently, remaining silent.

At last, I raised my eyes to her. "You saw this."

Pana'a looked to the lake before answering. "I did, Marareta."

"Yet you said nothing to me, nothing to Rahaita."

"Who was I to deny you your happiness, brief though it might be?"

"What shall I do?" I asked her. "What shall I do?"

"You will marry Panoha and have a daughter. Name her Rahiri. Visit me when you can."

The moon shone on A'auwa.

An Afterword

So concludes the story of Michael Malvern, Marareta, the Hero from the Sea. Of him, there would be little more to tell, for he lived a peaceful life among the Mora, honored by all, and had perhaps even found his place.

There is, of course, a son, and those have ways of finding their own adventures. Could some Mora storyteller have taken the time to compose an epic about them?

Stephen Brooke

Author and artist Stephen Brooke lives and works in an old farmhouse in the Florida Panhandle. All his books are available from Arachis Press, a small publisher dedicated to presenting meaningful literature for readers of all ages.

Visit http://arachispress.com for our catalog.

www.ingramcontent.com/pod-product-compliance
Lightning Source LLC
Chambersburg PA
CBHW030246030726
47493CB00023B/870